Birch Bentley:
Lies That Glitter - Book 1

He Wants It All...It Burns In His Soul

By Walt Bernard

(Note: It is highly recommended to read the Birch Bentley series of books in order)

Send questions or thoughts you may have to walt@waltbernard.com.

Published By: iPROFICIENCY www.iPROFICIENCY.com

Preface

You have enough ordinary in your life. Now step into Birch Bentley's world.

Birch Bentley is age 36 and is the #3 man in a large multi-billion dollar insurance company located in NYC.

He struggles to unseat two greedy insiders in an attempt to become President of the insurance company only to see a new, more powerful and cunning antagonist enter the picture.

He's handsome, and smart enough to see right through the lies of everyone around him, but he's blind to the lies that he tells, including the lies he tells to himself.

His business triumphs are threatened by his multiple love interests which end in tragedy, forcing him to finally see his faults - but it's too late.

If you are a person who thinks a lot about your goals and career, you will be pulled in by the harsh realities, messages, and truths that can be learned from Birch Bentley's story.

The characters expose something we should understand about our own behavior and those who we know and interact with. When we begin to discern that the face people show us is a mask; that what people are saying is not necessarily what they're thinking, we are finally prepared to deal with life as it is.

The Birch Bentley series draw you into the veracity of our lives, revealing the lesson of human destruction that can result from the obsessive chase for sex, wealth, and power. The insights unmask the unspoken realities about the corporate and social culture in which we live.

I recently heard someone say that one of his most enjoyable moments is when he finishes a book, puts it down, and says "*wow*." You'll be the judge if the book has "*wowed*" you; but that was my ambition.

Martha Carr, author of *"The List"* has written: *"books have their own power to transform. A book will take you on an adventure whenever you're ready."*

Enjoy the adventure.

Sol Stein set up my goal for this book with his statement that: *"a book should produce an experience superior to what we have in everyday life."*

Relish the experience.

I believe a book should draw you into a story that causes you to *feel* and *think*. If it can also be *fun* and *entertaining* you've hit a grand slam.

I've tried hard to give readers that journey. I've written the kind of book I would like to read, however, you are the ultimate judge of how I've done. I look forward to your feedback at walt@waltbernard.com.

As Napoleon Hill wrote; *"it is always your next move."*

Best wishes,

Walt Bernard

Notes:

There's a question of how much erotica, if any, should be included in a book. Great care has been applied to balance the sex; in as tasteful way as possible, with the same weight and manner the character would give it; and the reality of our society - no more, no less. For those of you who want to make a judgment ahead of time, you may consider if this book were a movie it would be rated "PG."

You may be interested in the back story of all the quotes attributed to Birch Bentley – the "Bentleyisms." They are either made up by the author, or adaptations of common phrases and thoughts, designed to enhance a particular segment from the story.

Settings from the books include exotic locations like: NYC, The Hamptons, Monaco, Santa Fe, Paris, Shanghai, Hawaii, and Boca del Toro, Panama.

Walter Bernard (Podgurski) entered the insurance business after graduating from Miami University of Ohio where he was an All-American wrestler and later was voted into the Miami University Athletic Hall-Of-Fame

The great majority of his experience is in voluntary employee benefit plans and publishing.

In 1997, Mr. Podgurski formed Insurance Broadcasting and the Workplace Benefits Association. In February 2011 Mr. Podgurski sold those assets to a major print publisher and event company.

Mr. Podgurski and his wife Betsy now live part of the year near Cleveland, Ohio and part of the year in Saint Augustine, Florida.

Birch Bentley Series 1 - 6

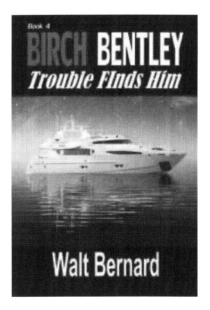

Book 5

BIRCH BENTLEY
Billionaire Bonus

Walt Bernard

Book 6

BIRCH BENTLEY
Chinese Dagger

Walt Bernard

TABLE OF CONTENTS

Birch Bentley: Lies That Glitter – Book 1
He wants it all; it burns in his soul.

2-13 - - The Sacrificing Of Brad Bishop
2-14 - - Vince Carter
2-15 - - Sandy Lockheart
2-16 - - The Politics Of Regulation

3: **The Hamptons -** Birch get's a taste of what life is going to be like if he makes it to the top.

3-1 - - The Invitation
3-2 - - The Move
3-3 - - The Missus
3-4 - - The Billionaire
3-5 - - A Lowly Caretaker
3-6 - - Social Graces
3-7 - - The Gift
3-8 - - The Reward
3-9 - - Jennifer Sable
3-10 - - Jacqueline Hightower

4: **Slaying The Dragons -** Birch is set up to take the fall but sometimes you must kill or be killed.

4-1 - - The One Thing
4-2 - - Sumptuosity
4-3 - - Making Trouble & Pointing Fingers
4-4 - - Mischief
4-5 - - Mood Change
4-6 - - Bull Charge
4-7 - - PAC Relief
4-8 - - Settle, No Matter What
4-9 - - A Botch Of Epic Proportions
4-10 - - Slaying The Dragons
4-11 - - The Board
4-12 - - Al Perri
4-13 - - Scott Kerr
4-14 - - One Final Thing To Do

1) It Burns In My Soul

1-1 - - Stunningly Beautiful Women And Making Money

"Right now my focus is on stunningly beautiful women and making money." - - Birch Bentley

I walked out onto an empty Park Avenue at 2:00 a.m. and nodded at the doorman.

"Do you think you can call me a cab?" I said to him

Before he could respond I was approached by four men. Their dark suits contrasted with their luminous white shirts. One of them showed me his badge.

I've always thought it was strange that badges have so much power over people. You can buy a decent one on the Internet for less than $30.00.

1

Before he could respond I was approached by four men. Their dark suits contrasted with their luminous white shirts. One of them showed me his badge.

"Mr. Bentley, I'm Special Agent Miller. Do you mind if I ask you a few questions?"

He knew my name, so this was not random. I looked at the four faces surrounding me. I had limited options.

"Guess not, go ahead." I shrugged.

"Not here, down at my office."

Whatever it was, I had nothing to worry about that I knew of.

"It's 2:00 a.m. I need to go home and get some sleep. Can't you just ask them here?"

"Not really; Mr. Bentley, we can do this the hard way or the easy way. It's up to you."

"Your office is the *easy* way?"

"Yes."

"Okay, if you've got coffee down there we can go, but let me see your I.D. again."

The information on his I.D. card said he was Special Agent Miller with the F.B.I. It looked real. Who else would be stopping me at this time of night?

There were two cars with drivers waiting at the street. That made six people assigned to whatever this was.

"I'm sorry, Mr. Bentley; I have to frisk you before we get in the car. It's procedure."

Miller sat in the front of the first car and I was sandwiched in the back seat between two of the others. The fourth went in the second car.

In the car there was no conversation. They probably wanted to give me my Miranda rights in their office while it was being videotaped.

The offices were much better that what you see on television. Lots of glass walls, clean desks. The conference room rivaled our extravagant board room. It had dark gray walls with recessed lighting that gave the walls an interesting texture, which served as a replacement for the lack of any art on the walls. The conference table and chairs weren't that upscale, but overall the effect was that of a professional and corporate environment.

I looked around for the one-way mirror, but if there was one there I couldn't find it. I did see two cameras, so I figured they probably used a video feed and didn't need the one-way glass anymore.

"Black," I said.

"Excuse me?" Miller asked with a questioning look on his face.

"I'll take my coffee black."

"The coffee is brewing. It'll be here in a minute."

"You're not a suspect in anything, Mr. Bentley but it's procedure to give you your Miranda rights."

He told me about my right to an attorney, but he didn't have to. I knew better than to answer any questions of substance without an attorney present. I'm well aware that it's a favorite trick of law enforcement to get you to say something, anything, and then use it to threaten perjury later. Law enforcement plays this 'extract information' game every day for a living.

"Now, let's start with your complete name."

"You brought me down here and you don't even know my full name?"

"We have a complete file on you, Mr. Bentley."

"Then you *know* it's Birch Bentley."

"What do you do, Mr. Bentley? For a living?"

"I'm senior vice president with Affluent Society Insurance."

"Big firm."

I couldn't tell if he was impressed or just blandly stating the obvious.

"We're trying to make it bigger."

"Tell me about the girl you were with tonight." He switched tacks abruptly.

"Is that what this is about? A gentleman doesn't kiss and tell."

"Mr. Bentley, we're all tired. Just answer the questions. Where did you meet her?"

"I met her at the Red Siren."

"Is that a bar?"

"Yes, in SoHo."

"Tonight?"

"No, a week ago. We had a dinner date tonight."

"What did she tell you about herself?"

"She works for a bank here in New York. She moved here from Paris about a year ago."

"What does she want from you?"

"What do you mean?"

"I mean has she asked you to do anything connected with your work?"

"Like what?"

"Like anything?"

"No."

"Did she tell you that her last boyfriend has been missing for almost a month?"

"I didn't ask her about her last boyfriend."

"Do you have anything to do with overseas transfers at Affluent Society?"

"They're one of the areas that I supervise, yes."

"Her last boyfriend, the one that is missing. He supervised overseas transfers at his organization as well."

"And?"

"And he approved a number of overseas transfers for your new girlfriend and now he's missing."

"Well, I haven't done any type of business transaction with her."

"We didn't say you did, but we think she's going to ask you to."

"Look, we have very strict compliance practices set up that adhere to all laws, including the Patriot Act. I know something about compliance because it's the department where I started with the company. We would never do any type of money transfer that crossed the line of legality."

We were right at the point where I wasn't going to answer any more questions without getting an attorney, even though that may have meant they would keep me there for an extended period of time.

"You said the word patriot, Mr. Bentley. Are you a patriot?"

"I served my country, five years, between college and law school."

"Yes. We checked you out last week when you went back to her place after meeting her. You had a very impressive record in the service."

"Thanks."

"You're in a unique position to be of help, Mr. Bentley. You have a distinguished record of service to your country, and you're involved with a woman we have a particular interest in."

"Well you can *have* her, because I lost my interest in her about sixty seconds ago.

"We want you to work with us, help us find out more about the operation she's involved in."

I thought for a minute about what he was asking.

"That's not going to happen, for several reasons."

"Tell me."

"Look, we're in the middle of a big acquisition. I'm only the third in line on the organization chart, and I would have to discuss something like this with the president and CEO. Trust me - they are not going to want the FBI anywhere near *anything* to do with the company right now. And if I do anything to screw up the acquisition, I can kiss my career goodbye."

"We only want you to get some information, Mr. Bentley."

"I know how this works. First you want some information. Then you'll be telling me to let an overseas transfer go through that violates the Patriot Act, or some law, so you can trace it. Then the shit will hit the fan somehow, the acquisition will blow up because big money doesn't like scrutiny, and I'll be looking for a new job,

kicking myself for being an idiot and agreeing to work with you in the first place."

"You've been watching a lot of television, haven't you?"

"I watch enough to see that the rat always ends up in the trap."

"You wouldn't be a rat, Mr. Bentley, you would be a hero."

"I have two bosses who I can assure you wouldn't see it that way. Can I go now, because I am through with the girl and through with any possibility of working as an informant?"

1-2 - - A Chance Meeting?

"A chance meeting isn't always a chance." - - Birch Bentley

I looked at my watch. To give myself the best chances of success I estimated I would have to block a two hour window of time between 8:30 a.m. and 10:30 a.m. Sunday morning.

When I arrived at Starbucks it was all clear.

I had chosen two of the big overstuffed brown chairs they have in every Starbucks in the U.S. I nudged them both about a foot closer to the wall to make them as far out of the earshot of others as possible. I reached in my bag and put some books and magazines on the chair across from me. I put some more on the blonde wood table in-between the two chairs and I put my bag down by my feet in order to move it up on my chair when the time came.

I ordered a Venti Pike Place and sat down with my iPad while I waited for what I wanted to see, mentally running through the timing and the planned sequence of events.

I kept watch on the sidewalk outside, and when I saw what I wanted I rose up from my seat, walked over to the area where you fix your drink, and poured the half of my coffee that was remaining into the hole in the center of the counter.

I had practiced the timing of this maneuver with other customers on different occasions, noting the exact time it took someone to reach the end of the serving line from the door and the number of seconds it took me to arrive from the milk and cream counter. My training emphasized the importance of rehearsal and this was too important to screw it up.

With my back half-turned to the order line I stood by in readiness. With the precision of a well planned military operation, I managed to arrive at the end of the line at the exact moment necessary to position myself behind my target.

I scanned the line in front of me. There were six customers with two clerks taking orders. Just my luck the one time the line would be short was when I wanted it to be long. I was going to have to work faster than I wanted to.

"Excuse me," I said to the woman who had just arrived. "I think we might live in the same building. On 37th?"

This wasn't the best opening I ever came up with, but it held enough affinity to get the conversation started. She turned around to look at me and her eyes were a pool of bright blue, contrasted by her jet black hair. I thought she might be Italian or Middle-Eastern. She radiated a physical strength despite her petite body and delicate facial features. Probably in her late twenties, she was a rose in full bloom, at the peak of her beauty.

She was wearing black leggings, a tan winter jacket, and she had one of those long knit scarves that you can wrap around yourself a couple of times if you want. Her hat matched her scarf and her brown shoes matched her purse.

I had seen her in our building foyer with her coat unbuttoned and knew her top half equaled the sexy legs that projected like two pedestals of sensuality from the bottom of her coat.

"Yes, that's my building. Have you lived there long?" she asked me.

8

I was disappointed that she didn't acknowledge she recognized me. Was she playing it coy? We had made eye contact at least twice in the past two weeks.

"Just a month or so. I thought now would be a good time to buy because prices are going up again. How about you?"

"I just moved in a few weeks ago. I moved here from Atlanta to jumpstart my literary career."

The building we lived in was on the expensive side for someone just starting out. I looked down at her left hand and there was no ring. Maybe she had family money.

It was time for phase two of my plan and we were already at the pastries, ice teas, and juices case.

I looked down pretending to be studying the orange juices and asked her name in the most casual manner I could manage.

"Since we're neighbors, we should probably know each other's names. My name is Birch."

I reached down and pulled out an orange juice to drink along with my Venti Pike Place refill

"I've never met a Birch before."

Her face radiated curiosity as she spoke the words. You could almost see her brain sorting through the consequences of having a name like Birch.

"My mother named me Birch. She was, actually still is, a throwback hippie who loves everything earthy. She liked to tease me and claim her second choice was Branch."

"Was her third choice Twig?"

All the people I've told that story to about my mother teasing me with 'Branch,' and nobody was ever quick enough to come back with a 'Twig' reference.

"I guess I'm lucky she stopped at Birch. And you are?"

"Susan - my mother was a WASP."

This girl knew how to keep the references in play. I took her engagement with me as a sign she wanted to keep the conversation going. That, plus the fact that she had turned around to face me rather than looking at the cashier, were the kind of clues I was looking for.

"There's probably a joke there about a tree, and a wasp in the tree, if I was more clever, but I can't think of one right now. You mentioned literary career. Are you an author or agent?

"I work for a publishing company. I'm trying to work my way up to literary agent. How about you?"

"I work for Affluent Society Insurance. Have you heard of it?"

"Of course! Everybody knows Affluent Society Insurance. I see their ads everywhere. Upscale service for everyone; is that how it goes?"

"You nailed it. I'm impressed. I was just promoted to Executive Vice-President reporting directly to the President. About four months ago."

"May I take your order?"

From the way we were standing and talking the cashier guessed we were together and directed her question to both of us.

"Susan, let *me* pay. As a way of saying thanks for standing in line with me and helping me celebrate my promotion."

"Okay, I'll let you pay, if we can sit down for a minute and talk about your new job. It sounds a lot more exciting than mine.

Of course we were going to sit down and talk. That was why I had claimed the two brown chairs with my magazines and books.

"You wouldn't believe. It's probably a good idea to do a little celebrating now."

"Why?"

"The people in my job before me have lasted about as long as the average NFL kickoff returner. Let's just say 'not for long' doesn't only apply to the National Football League. You're riding high as a superstar one day and the next day, not so much."

Once we sat down the conversation went on for a long time. She was dredging information out of me that I hardly ever talked about.

"I didn't have the problems in the military I have in business. I lived by a credo. Serve with honor and integrity, loyalty to country; defeat our nation's enemies, and more. Once you take off the uniform, put on a suit, and step into the business world, you find out that commerce isn't played with the same set of rules."

"How so, Birch?"

"In business the bad guys don't shoot back with bullets, they shoot back with lies and deceit. When they *'take you out'* it's not *'capping your ass'* it's *'canning your ass.'*

"Did you think about staying in the service?"

"Not really, what I like about industry is you can make money, lots of it. I developed my own set of rules."

"Are they something you can share?"

"I don't share them often, but I think I can make an exception for you. I live by 5 very simple rules."

'Don't get hurt.'

'Don't hurt anyone else that doesn't have it coming to them.'

'Try not to break anything.'

'Don't do anything illegal.'

'*Have fun.*'

"That keeps it simple for me so I don't have to over think anything. Kind of like when I was in the military."

1-3 - - Susan

I had a feeling I would see that hunk that moved into our apartment building at Starbucks one day. I never saw him without a Starbucks in his hand. I pretended like I had never noticed him.

When he stood in line behind me, I knew he would be making a move. He didn't have to try hard to get my attention. That was why I was there in the first place.

I was surprised how easy it was to talk to him. We talked for almost two hours. He asked me what I was going to be doing the rest of the day but hold on big boy, I'm not that easy. I don't care how rich or good looking you are.

Let's see what other moves he has.

1-4 - - Special Agent Miller

"To be GOVERNED is to be watched, inspected, spied upon, directed, law-driven, numbered, regulated, enrolled, indoctrinated, preached at, controlled, checked, estimated, valued, censured, commanded, by creatures who have neither the right nor the wisdom nor the virtue to do so." - - Pierre-Joseph Proudhon (French) 1809 - 1865

That week I was sitting in my office when my assistant, Sean, interrupted me.

"Birch, there's a Special Agent Miller down in the lobby who wants to see you."

That son-of-a-bitch Miller thought he could come to my office and put some pressure on me. He knew full well that I wouldn't

want to be seen with an FBI agent at my office. There is no possible way for that to be a good thing.

The government has too much access. They pry into anything they want and use it to stomp on anybody they want.

Sean could be trusted to never mention it, but whoever was working the security desk downstairs now knew, and those guys talked a lot.

"Call down and let the front desk know I'll be right down."

I went downstairs to our reception desk where Miller was waiting. Walking over to where he sat, I warmly greeted him and shook his hand.

"Special Agent Miller, how nice of you to drop by unannounced in the middle of the work day."

I hoped he appreciated the nuances of what I was telling him.

"Your timing is excellent. I wasn't that busy, so I was just about to take a long coffee break. There's a Starbucks right next door. Would you like to join me?"

There was no way I was taking him up to my office.

We ordered some coffee and sat down in as private a place as we could find.

"Mr. Bentley, have you given any more thought to our conversation the other night?"

"Not one bit, sir."

"That's unfortunate. I talked to one of your superiors when you were in the service, Major Underwood. Do you remember him?"

"Of course I remember him."

"He said you were the kind of Marine who would never back away from any assignment, regardless of how tough it was."

"That was then and this is now. I have the same fighting spirit, but I have different priorities now."

"Your new girlfriend is probably wondering why you haven't called."

"She can keep wondering."

"I don't think she's the type to wonder for too long. If you don't call her she's going to be calling you. I'm sure you realize by now that she targeted you."

"Really? You don't think it was my good looks and charm?"

"Remember I told you that her last boyfriend went missing?"

"Sort of, I'm trying to remember. Oh yeah, I think that may have had something to do with my decision to stop seeing her."

"He's still missing."

"Thanks for the update."

"He had a family, a wife and three kids."

"I'm sorry for their loss if he is truly missing."

"Here's the point, Mr. Bentley, Her group is dangerous and you're on their radar now. Don't you think it would be better to cooperate with us and let us protect you?"

"Like you protected the missing guy? I might go out and get a gun and a gun permit. I've been thinking about that anyhow."

"Just continue seeing her for awhile. When we have enough evidence we'll swoop down on them and put them away for good."

"You know what I just heard? I swear it sounded to me like you want me to wear a wire. Don't you watch television Special Agent Miller? The guy wearing the wire always ends up in some serious shit."

"You're already in some serious shit. You just don't realize it."

"The answer is no. Next time, and I sincerely hope there is no next time, don't just stop by my office. It doesn't help either one of us to have someone from the FBI showing up to see me. I'll write down my cell phone number for you. Call me, and if we have to meet I'll meet you here."

"No need, Mr. Bentley, I already have your cell number."

1-5 - - A Liar and a Cheat

"Here's to alcohol, the rose colored glasses of life." - - F. Scott Fitzgerald, The Beautiful and Damned

The following Friday I was in my favorite seat, 1B, waiting for the plane to board on a flight home to New York City from a conference in St. Louis. My thoughts were interrupted by a pretty flight attendant.

"Here's your wine, sir."

I looked up and locked my eyes on hers. As she reached over to put my Chardonnay on my armrest we studied each other's faces for a second longer than most people do,

"And for you, sir, Crown Royal with a side of water." She reached across me to hand Al Perri his beverage and I could smell her perfume.

I looked to my left and observed a man who was a liar, a cheat, and the President of Affluent Society Insurance Company.

If you caught him unaware, just staring and thinking, he looked a bit smug. Once aware of your presence, however, he became the master of charm. Only the most perceptive could see through his masquerade.

Al Perri was not only sitting in the seat next to me, he sat in the next job I wanted. I was obsessed with plans to hasten his exit. Some would consider it disloyal to purposefully displace your

mentor. Loyalty was a two-way street, however, and Al Perri had no loyalty to anybody but himself. I was only planning to do to Al what he had been doing to other people his entire life.

At fifty-six he was twenty years older than me. The conventional advice was to be patient and wait my turn.

Bullshit. Waiting your turn was last generation.

As far as I was concerned it was my turn right now, and not just as the president of the company, it was my turn to be the CEO.

Perri and our CEO didn't deserve to have their jobs. They did nothing to improve the company, except possibly the acquisition we were working on, and rake in every bit of compensation and perks for themselves they could.

As the passengers in coach started to board I took a sip of my Chardonnay — not a great Chardonnay, too much oak, but at least it was cold.

My attention shifted to sexy Sandy Lockheart as I watched her come through the cabin door.

"Hello, Mr. Bentley. I see we'll be on the same plane back," Sandy said in a warm tone.

It occurred to me that if Al hadn't insisted we stay in the airline club drinking until the last moment, I could have been chatting Sandy up in the boarding area.

Sandy was at the same conference Al and I were attending. She held her tote bag jammed with folders and brochures the way you would carry a football.

In her early thirties, Sandy Lockheart worked in the compliance department of Affluent Society. That was the department I started in out of law school, but I transferred out before Sandy started there.

"Sandy, it looks as if you're taking most of the conference back to New York with you."

"I'm going to sort through it all on the way back."

Al Perri leaned into me slightly "Have you hit her yet?"

I cringed at the sound of Al's voice, too loud for the togetherness of an airplane cabin. Sandy, only a few rows away, may even have heard him. I wanted to turn around to see if she had heard and reacted, but if she saw me turning it would have been worse.

Al was so used to overpowering everybody and everything that it sometimes made him situational unaware. His attitude was others could adjust to him, not he should adjust to them. People that are as smooth as Al can get away with pretty much anything. They don't have to think ahead because they are brilliant at improvising as they go along.

This was completely opposite from my training which was to always be aware of all aspects of your environment so that the maximum odds were in your favor, an extension of the overwhelming force principle.

I leaned in to Al. *"Not even close, Al,"* I said at a barely audible volume.

I hoped he would get the clue that maybe our conversation should be more discreet in the close quarters of first class. We were talking about a female employee in a sexual way. I wasn't about to have my career halted by carelessly making some offhand comment and find myself in a sexual harassment turmoil.

What I was thinking, however, was that I had heard she was in the middle of a divorce.

"Birch, why don't we put her on the M&A team and take her with us on a visit to ALH? Put her in a short skirt, or a pants suit with a low neckline sweater. That's the way to make an impression."

ALH was Arkansas Life & Health. Affluent Society Insurance was trying to acquire ALH. If the transaction went through, everyone at the top stood to realize substantial gains on their stock options and get rich. In reality the only one who would 'get

rich' would be me. Everyone else, Donald Hightower, our CEO, Perri, our board of directors, our institutional investors; they were already rich and would just be getting richer.

Al was right about adding an attractive woman to our team. It would at least gain attention, if not respect. There was no reason not to capitalize on the deference people give to beauty.

Still in my quiet, inside first-class voice, I leaned over to Al again and said, *"You know Ramsey Lane can afford to have all the women like Sandy he wants."*

Ramsey Lane was the chairman of ALH. Our research showed his net worth was over one hundred million. He was almost mythical in some circles with folklore stories of his rag to riches rise an iconic illustration of what you could achieve with hard work and brains.

I thought for a moment about what Donald Hightower, Al Perri, and Ramsey Layne would think if they found out I was cooperating with the FBI. Does Miller have any clue at all about how people at that level think?

"Yeah," Al went on in a voice still too loud, "But guys like that never get close to sweet stuff like Sandy. Society has boxed in people that live in a small town like Little Rock. In a closed society; only the really cagey can find a way to have their family, company, position, and also manage to have a private nookie stash on the side."

Why do people from New York, people like Al, think everywhere else is Hicksville? Al did know about managing something on the side. He was the most notorious womanizer I had ever seen and I had witnessed some guys in the service with gargantuan appetites for female company.

The man sitting across the aisle to our right turned and looked at us with a half-disgusted face when Al used the nookie word.

Al leaned forward with a *"can I help you?"* look and the man went back to the paper he was reading.

That should have ended it, but Al wasn't about to let it go. He leaned forward even more and gave him the look a second time like people from New York do. When Al still didn't get a response he added a small amount of *'you want some of this?'* body language to a third attempt to engage the man across from us.

What a joke. Al wasn't a fighter. If Al went up against somebody who knew what they were doing, in less time than it takes to say *'let's go'* he'd be either dead or in the hospital for a month. He had a fighter's attitude but he didn't have anything physically to back it up.

Sometimes watching Al reminded me of those anole lizards that puff up their throat and dance around each other. It's all an act of intimidation and show. A lot of what Al achieved was accomplished strictly with attitude.

The flight attendant who was standing in the galley directly in front of us came over. As an experienced flight attendant she most likely had a sense of who had consumed too much alcohol before boarding.

"Is everything okay?" she asked in a low key manner so as not to add to add to the tension.

"Absolutely," I replied waving her off.

Fortunately, the man to our right continued to stare at his book and Al became re-engaged in our conversation.

"Did you see the absurd amount of paper she was carrying from the conference?" Al asked me.

Al was still talking too loud, but at least the subject now had nothing to do with sex.

"Sandy's still in the ideas and information stage of her career, Al; we all have to go through it."

"Somebody should straighten her out. Information and degrees aren't going to get people to where they want to go; it's relationships, but people don't want to hear that. They'd rather

19

borrow $150,000 to go to school and graduate with a loan that will take years to pay back."

This, from a man with a MBA from NYU.

Al downed his Crown Royal. "Do you see the flight attendant? I need a refill before we take off. Quarterly earnings get reported today and they aren't going to be what they should be."

I couldn't believe Al was going to ask for another drink before we even got off the ground, but that was Al. If airlines could measure how many drinks you had before you got on the airplane, Al would never be able to fly anywhere.

The amount of alcohol he drank would be the downfall of most people, but Al rarely showed the effects of what he knocked back.

1-6- - Al Perri

Birch Bentley is a little big for his britches, but I keep him close because he's useful. He thinks he's my understudy but he's more like my lackey, the corporate equivalent of domestic help.

People like him think they're indispensable and on their way to the top, right up to the moment when they get their ass terminated.

1-7 - - $2.00 Can Get You Fired

"Even small matters can translate into life or death." - - Birch Bentley

"Man, it's cold out there, even for January," Al said as we got into the limo at JFK.

I looked at my messages and centered on one from my assistant Sean. *'call me...important.'*

Sean picked up my call on the first ring.

"Sean, what's so important? Depending on traffic I'm about 40 minutes away."

"Quarterlies were reported today. Revenues and profits missed expectations by a mile. The stock tanked around 4%."

I must have made a face.

"What?" asked Al.

I put my hand over the telephone.

"Sean says we missed our quarterly numbers and the market shaved close to two dollars off our share price."

"*Son of a bitch!* Hightower personally lost a half-million dollars today. He's going to be intolerable" Al said. "He's going to need to blow off some steam. In theory, the company is worth eighty-million less this afternoon than it was this morning."

Donald Hightower was our highly volatile CEO. Al didn't mention his own stock, but the losses on his options were severe as well.

"Al, the stock will go back up and the company is still, more or less, worth $1 billion."

"Birch, do you like working for Affluent Society? If you do I wouldn't share that mindset around Hightower."

Donald Hightower's whimsical firings were legendary. Either he already fired most of the senior talent, or they left before he could fire them. Up to now this worked in my favor. Every time Hightower fired somebody it created an opening and eliminated one more person between me and the job I wanted, which was Al Perri's and then Hightower's after that.

Al was my buffer from Hightower, because Al liked having me around to support his drinking and chasing.

When we arrived at our midtown Manhattan office building, I left my luggage downstairs with security and went up to my floor. Sean stopped me outside my office.

"Mr. Hightower wants to see you and Al Perri right now."

I could hear Hightower ranting and raving through the boardroom's glass walls as soon as I stepped off the elevator. I knew I was in for another one of those meetings that are extremely dangerous from a career perspective.

Hightower was unpredictable which is what made it a treacherous setting. I had never seen it but I had heard stories of him firing people on the spot.

One of Hightower's assistants gave me my instructions.

"Go right in, Mr. Bentley. Mr. Perri is already inside."

Al had been quick to arrive for the meeting. He occupied a big office just one floor below. When Hightower became CEO, he'd cleared the entire top floor; one-half for his oversized office and his staff, the other half for an impressive board room.

As I came to understand Hightower, I realized he was a private person who valued his solitude immensely. That side of him, combined with his temper, added to his complexity. I tiptoed around Donald Hightower and remained out of his sight as much as I could.

Everyone has their own burden. Hightower's was his volatility. I imagined that at home his family walked around on eggshells the same as we did here at the office. People's vulnerabilities and personality disorders follow them wherever they go.

How people with major foibles like Hightower and Perri get to be at the top of their organizations, which is not uncommon, perplexed me. My intensive study of leaders and leadership offered no clues to explain how the biggest a-holes with the least talent always seem to dominate the highest management positions.

I didn't even have a chance to sit down at the meeting before Hightower was asking me questions. I was sure he'd already bullied everyone else there, and my arrival presented him with a fresh target.

"Birch, marketing is part of your responsibilities, right? What kind of crappy job are the salespeople doing out there?"

Sales had actually moved up for the quarter, but that wasn't going to appease Hightower at that particular moment. Instead of answering, I sat down pretending he had asked a rhetorical question. He often moved from person to person posing questions that he really meant as statements.

"I asked you a question, Birch," Hightower ground out in a menacing tone that demanded an answer.

My finesse hadn't worked so I tried a second one.

"I'm sorry, Mr. Hightower. I was going to pull out my iPad and double-check the sales results before I responded."

"Birch, you should know those kind of numbers without having to look them up."

He was right about that. I had slipped up with my dodgy response. I should have given him the numbers and taken any flak.

He didn't wait for me to pull out my iPad. He turned his head to address Dave Bress, the head of our investor relations department.

"Dave, how did the projections get so far ahead of our numbers? You're supposed to be managing what the analysts are expecting."

Dave looked down sheepishly then looked back up.

"We had some late reversals. I wasn't made aware of the losses in time to do anything about them from an expectation perspective."

Offering a lame excuse like that was a potentially unsafe response when Hightower was shaking with anger.

"We pay you to anticipate reversals, Dave. Did you just start here last week?"

Without waiting for Dave to answer he banged the table and picked on our CFO, Cathy Black.

"Cathy, if we had reversals, why weren't some of the expenses deferred until next quarter? How hard can delaying a few payments be for crying out loud? Do I have to come down to accounting and look at the spreadsheets myself?"

Cathy had been through this scene before; she looked more perplexed than intimidated. A long-time employee, she knew CEO's come and they go.

"There are certain things that can't be deferred without doing more long-term harm than good," Cathy responded.

Cathy was the only one who dared to even hint at a retort to one of Hightower's questions. Under the circumstances this was the equivalent of an '*in your face*' showdown.

Al Perri had an irritating knack for putting himself above the discussion by aligning himself with Hightower and bundling the rest of us as screw-ups who weren't worthy of our jobs.

"Folks, a surprise like missing our numbers is unacceptable. The only way that could happen is if our reporting systems are dysfunctional. Going forward I want a review of how we track our quarterly numbers, and I want one person accountable for monitoring the key ratios and communicating them to everyone else." Al told the group.

Wonderful, genius, I thought. Why didn't you come up with that brilliant idea before the numbers came in so bad and the stock nosedived? Did you just start here last week? Al should have just gotten up and kissed Hightower's ass, it would have been more dignified.

Scott Kerr, our corporate communications director, was another aggravating person. He would always include someone else's name in whatever he had to say and make it sound like that

person said it first. Or he would take something that somebody said and twist it as evidence for what he himself was saying, even if there was zero connection between what the other person said and Scott's point.

Do the douches go to douche school somewhere to learn this kind of behavior? Is there a *'Being A Douche For Dummies'* book they all read in middle school, the new young adult best seller?

When Scott Kerr does this I have to squelch calling him out on it, but Hightower seemed to like the guy so I just kept my mouth shut. When you work in a large corporation there are some things you just have to swallow.

I doubted whether many in the room, other than Hightower, considered a $2.00 stock fluctuation a life-or-death matter. Nobody wanted to see the stock drop in price, but we all knew the value of the stock we owned was a roller coaster ride. Of course, none of the rest of us owned a quarter of a million shares. Maybe I was being too harsh a judge. Maybe a half-million dollar swing in net worth from day-to-day would put anybody on edge.

Hightower made his way back to me.

"Birch, do you have those sales numbers yet?"

"Yes, we were up 1.5% from the same quarter a year earlier."

"That's deplorable, Birch.

Deplorable? Doesn't he know we're in a low growth economy? Other companies are losing market share and we're increasing ours.

Hightower stopped and looked around the room. Nobody wanted his eyes to stop on them so everybody had their head lowered as if they were in prayer. Some of us may have actually been in prayer that we wouldn't be fired.

Hightower threw out a theoretical question that only his great intellectual capacity would even be able to contemplate let alone have an answer for.

"Do I have to remind everyone that we're trying to transact an acquisition and our currency is our stock price? Am I the *only* one that gets that?"

Nobody volunteered an answer to his questions. Hightower threw his hands in the air and then towards the door.

"All of you, get out of here."

Wow, even for Hightower this was an abrupt end to a meeting. Apparently the acquisition transaction had him strung tighter than a professional's tennis racket.

Al stopped me outside the conference room on the way out.

"Have a car pick us up downstairs at 6:00 p.m. and stay low-key the rest of the day. Somebody is going to find a pink slip on their desk when they arrive Monday morning, if they don't get it today."

"Should I be concerned, Al?"

"No, my guess is somebody from finance that works for Cathy will be scapegoated. The bean counters had the final opportunity to save the numbers and didn't. Cathy's not at risk because we can't afford to lose her."

'Hang 'Em Hightower' was about to keep his reputation intact and nobody was safe. Whether we could or couldn't afford to lose someone didn't seem to have mattered much in the past. When Hightower got into one of his unstable emotional states, everyone's neck was potentially on the chopping block.

This was the kind of instance when I was glad to be under Al's protection, but that was still no guarantee. It was entirely possible that I would look up at any time and see some security people who would watch me pack my things and escort me out of the building. That was why I brought my own iPad to work, keeping the receipt tucked inside the cover jacket.

It was ridiculous that my career was in a continually precarious position, largely because it was in the hands of two threatening

people; one who I considered unstable, and the other a user of people. This was why I had to unseat them before I became another victim of their dysfunctional ineptitude.

1-8 - - Donald Hightower

Unimportant, annoying, little people. There are so many of them. They have no idea of the responsibility I have. Three billion dollars under investment, four thousand employees, and two million policyowners are all affected by my decisions.

I'd like to be a nice guy and take a personal interest in each and every one of the toady subordinates, but that's impossible. I'm not going to make the effort to try and fake it. The trains have to run on time, said Mussolini, or chaos will ensue. I am the man in charge because I understand my duties and carry them out.

Yes, I fire people, but other people have to face up to their accountability the same as I do. In most cases I'm doing them a favor. They are either unsuited for the job they have or they need a slap in the face to get them awake to see reality and get back on track. They all find employment again. I haven't heard of any of them starving to death because of insufficient food and water. Nobody I've fired lives on the streets as far as I know. They are merely inconvenienced for awhile and are so at the fault of no one but themselves.

If they were to walk a mile in my shoes, they would see the necessity for the things I do.

That's why I keep my distance. I don't want to be their friend; I want to be the CEO of the insurance company they work for. A company that makes money and provides a fair service in exchange for the premiums that are charged.

They need to get a clue that we're not all in this together. The company cannot afford to fail and therefore I cannot afford to fail. If they don't get that, I'm sorry, but that may be one of the reasons they weren't appointed CEO.

I'll do my job, they can do their job, and if we never meet, fine with me. I want nothing from them other than their best possible

performance at work, and while they're at it, please stay away from me. I report to the Board and no one else.

1-9 - - Would You Like To Be A Pal with Al?

"Will you walk into my parlour?' said the Spider to the Fly." - - Mary Howitt (1799-1888)

That night Al and I went to a new trendy restaurant in SoHo. On a Friday night, Grazzi's would fill with impressionable women waiting for Mr. Moneybags to come along, scoop them up, marry them, and move them to Connecticut, or some exclusive part of Westchester County or upscale New Jersey.

Al and I had begun spending a lot of time together three years before this when he spotted me socializing with two lovely girls at a restaurant bar. Al assumed that one of those girls might be available to him. His good fortune turned out to be lucky for me as well.

A smart guy like Al figured out quickly that being paired up with a younger, better-looking guy could open doors to a duo of girls easier than he ever could on his own.

Al wanted to make sure I was readily available when he wanted to go drinking and chasing, which was three or four times a week. To keep me accessible, he put me in the company's "Fast Start" program and jumped me up the management line whenever he could.

My reputation as *'Al's boy'* helped me considerably. At the risk of appearing ungrateful it wasn't a label I wore proudly; it was only tactical. I was using my relationship with Al to get ahead, and as a shield for safety from Donald Hightower.

Men who find meeting women difficult could learn a lot from watching Al work a place like Grazzi's. Women could learn even more. Al's approach to women was identical to the way he approached life; deceive and take what he wanted.

Grazzi's had a circular bar in its center, and dining tables occupying the back half. Al liked to stand at the first bend in the

bar so that people had to walk past him to get to the rest of the bar or to the dining tables and restrooms.

Occupying this position gave him the opportunity to say hello to the ladies as they went to their tables or to powder their noses. He was also in the perfect position to watch the door. Al considered his spot to be the equivalent of a basketball player being *"in the paint."*

It didn't take long for two lovelies to come by. One of them glanced at Al as she approached. If a pretty girl made any kind of eye contact, Al was going to take a shot at inviting her to a conversation.

Al stuck out his hand for a handshake and delivered his favorite opening line.

"My name is Al, rhymes with pal. Would you like to be a pal with Al?"

The first time I heard him say that I thought *'You have got to be kidding me.'* He stops a woman mid-stride and delivers a hammy line like that? To my surprise, he reeled her in.

As I got to know Al better I saw his line had a method to its madness.

First, he was being proactive and wasn't waiting for someone else to initiate the action. That by itself put him ahead of half the men in the bar sitting around talking about what they would do if they got someone in bed rather than what they were actually going to do. A lot of girls kept walking but a lot stopped and talked. Al was unconditionally unafraid of rejection; completely fearless in this regard.

Second, I think he caught people off-guard with his manner. There is a certain attraction for a man with pizzazz who carries himself well in a confident manner. He had that same aura about him as when a doctor comes into the room where you're waiting, and asking you where it hurts. You immediately start telling a total stranger your most intimate details. Al knew what he was doing when it came to women and it showed.

29

Third, Al had a pattern to his conversation. He did what we all do, which is to find a way to work what we want to talk about into the conversation.

I see this on a regular basis. People always manage to work their talking points into their comments early: their kids, their hobbies, their work, their awards, their alma mater, their operation, their whatever. Within two or three minutes they've steered the conversation to include their big thing of the moment.

Why is it, for instance, that people think other people they hardly know want to hear about every detail of their medical history?

Al's pattern would be to draw women in with a ridiculous pickup line, work in how he used to travel all over the globe, and cap off his narrative by making sure they knew he was president of a big insurance company with a lavish lifestyle.

As I watched him work I thought his methods so seemingly transparent they wouldn't fool anybody. But to paraphrase a common saying, Al couldn't fool all of the women all of the time but he could fool some of the women some of the time. That was good enough for Al.

Al was waiting for an answer to his 'would you like to be a pal with Al?' question.

"Sure, why not?" she said.

Having initiated contact, the next step was to establish himself as a worldly person.

Still holding her hand, Al told her about where he had just been, setting up his global travels statement.

"I just got back today from a conference in St. Louis. I don't mind the trips to places like St. Louis, where I was this week. They are so much easier than the overseas trips."

This was Al's clue to her that he had traveled internationally.

"What kind of work do you do?" Al asked.

This question from Al would eventually lead to her asking what he did, so he could modestly tell her he was president of an insurance company.

"I'm in finance at a bond trading company. What do you do?"

"I'm the president of an insurance company, Affluent Society Insurance, have you heard of it?"

Of course she had; everybody in the U.S with a television had.

"Yes," she said, clearly impressed that she was speaking to the president of such a large and well-known company.

Al was audacious in his strategy and relentless in his pursuit. In less than three minutes after accepting Al's friendship offer, a woman would know he had traveled all over the world and was president of an insurance company.

Al left nothing to chance. He delivered his engineered script magnificently. Al had raised his performance to an art form; it was pure theatre.

Al had a quest — to get laid — and woe to the woman he drew in. He also had a motto; 'Three times and out' and he wasn't referring to dinners.

No one sees the hump on his own back. Al saw absolutely nothing wrong with drinking to excess, cheating on his wife, and taking advantage of women, or people in general for that matter.

1-10 - - Contact

"Meeting someone who is going to turn out to be special is something you realize immediately upon contact." - - Birch Bentley

As Al was exerting maximum effort with his new pal, someone cute kind of accidentally-on-purpose bumped against my arm.

"I'm not crowding you, am I?" she asked, like she had just noticed our close proximity.

I looked at her for a second. This was the same awesome girl that had been standing on the other side of the bar a few minutes ago. She had looked at me for a second and then gone back talking to another man at the bar. Now she was standing next to me and offered a conversation opening. It was game time and I felt a jolt of adrenaline.

"A little or so, I'll give you 15 minutes to stop. My name is Birch. Have we met?"

"Birch, like in the tree?"

"I get that a lot, yes."

"My name is Jennifer."

"Pleased to meet you, Jennifer. Out celebrating anything special tonight?"

"I just finished a reception for some incentive travel buyers. I wasn't quite ready to go home yet."

"Well, that was lucky for me. Can I refill whatever kind of wine that is you're drinking?"

I got the bartenders attention, pointed to Jennifer's glass and held up two fingers.

"Nice watch," she said. "Are you a pilot or a diver?"

Jennifer had noticed my Breitling. Not everybody knows their price tag, but those who do are impressed when they see one on my wrist. Expensive watches were one of the tools I used to create a persona of success without resorting to the pretentious conversation loop that Al Perri used.

Aside from its eye-catching appeal, my Breitling has the practical use of staying watertight to 1,650 feet, in case I'm ever at that depth and need to know the time.

"Neither," I said. "I prefer ground that is only slightly higher than sea level. I just like the way a Breitling looks. Are you familiar with them?"

"Sort of, I used to date a diver who wore one." She looked over at Al. "Your friend seems to be getting along well with his new friend."

"That's the President of our insurance company."

"Is that his wife?"

This was an unusual question although Al never hid the fact that he was married.

"No."

My answer created an awkward moment between Jennifer and I, but it was because her question was awkward.

"Is he married? He looks married."

This was another awkward question and I began to wonder if she was more interested in Al than she was in me. I was already starting to lose interest, how can someone look married?

"Jennifer, it's probably best to address that question some other time."

"I'll take that as a yes. His new friend doesn't seem to be concerned about whether he is or isn't."

It dawned on me that maybe she wasn't judging Al's behavior as much as she wanted to judge *my* reaction to Al's behavior.

I reconsidered my interest level. My lust radar was telling me this was a girl I should open up the throttle with if I wanted to stand out. She was most likely hit on several times a day and anything conventional would fall flat. She had a sixth sense and she wanted to know if I was like Al. Was I the kind of man that would lie, cheat, and deceive my partner?

I had my own script that I pulled out of my bag of tricks that would eventually lead up to the advice my mother would always give me.

"Jennifer, have you ever heard of smart seduction?"

No, but I think it's probably something I should hear about."

"A man, any man, not just Al, who wants to seduce a woman should never be crude, never step over the boundaries of acceptable behavior. He draws women in with his wit and builds the castle in the sky until they want to step into the world he's shaped. He frames the fantasy to dizzying levels, making the woman desperate to be a part of it. He's rich, traveled, goes to the nicest places, is funny; helps her understand all the things she will be missing out on without him, and most important of all, he should listen when a woman is talking."

"Is that what he's doing?" Jennifer asked me.

"I didn't say that. If you ask any woman you meet whether she would have an affair with a married man, you know the kind of look you would get. Yet how many women are having affairs with somebody's husband?"

"I've known women who have but I never would."

"Jennifer, many women who meet somebody that offers most, if not all, of what they need to fulfill their emotional and physical desires can become blind to what's missing or unfavorable. To borrow a term, they create a 'reality distortion field' around the man, in order to see what they want to see and only see that. The woman enjoys the sex, the attention, the gifts, the places they go, the things they do, and basking in the sphere of a powerful man. If that makes her happy, why not?

"I find that very sad, Birch."

"Niccolo Machiavelli said it best, 'a deceitful man will always find plenty who are ready to be deceived.'"

"That's also sad."

"Not to get overly dramatic, but there's another saying: *'Don't stick your head in a wolf's mouth.'*"

"It sounds like you have a million of them. Are you going to be here all week?"

"Sorry, Jennifer, I get a little carried away with all my quotes some of the time."

"Thanks for the warning about sticking my head in the wolf's mouth, I'll be sure to follow that advice. And what kind of seducer are *you*, Birch? Should I be concerned that you're a wolf as well, like your buddy over there?"

It didn't happen very often that I could have such a candid conversation the first time I met someone, but it did occasionally happen. It was usually when the other person was intelligent, and open, and somebody I thought I could become interested in. In those circumstances there was an excitement that built inside of me that was not just sexual, it was something more, something that woke up all my senses, pushing me to the brink of going over the line.

I was at that boundary. I pulled everything back to the safe zone and gave Jennifer the answer she wanted to hear. The one that set up the separation between me and all the other men Jennifer meets.

"The honest kind, Jennifer, who believes in transparency and trust. I don't judge anybody else's behavior; I just try to sort out the reality between what people do and what people say."

There was no reason to explain to Jennifer that I play my own games and I play to win. I simply stay as close to my rule #1 as I can — "I get what I want without anybody who doesn't deserve injury getting hurt."

The next thing for me to do was to separate myself one more level from the kind of man Al Perri was. Women love it when they think your Mom brought you up to respect girls.

"Do you know what my mother told me, Jennifer?"

"What?"

"My mother would say all the time: 'Don't play with a woman's heart.' If men followed this simple rule, they would stay out of a lot of trouble. Along with math and English, schools should teach it. Short of that, every mother should teach that practical wisdom to their sons. Mom had a little saying about 'don't make a girl fall if you don't plan to catch her.' I was in my teens before I fully understood what she meant."

"You sound a little egotistical, but your Mom sounds like a very wise woman, Birch."

"She's a northern California hippie who loves all things earthy. She's the one who named me Birch."

I did receive that solid advice from my mother. I just wasn't above using it for my benefit when the opportunity presented itself. It could be true and also be a useful tool to create a perception.

1-11 - - Al Perri

I don't see what the problem is with other people. Life is like a candy store and I take what I want. I've got plenty of money, I drink plenty of alcohol, and I get plenty of girls. Most men would envy that kind of lifestyle if they were honest with themselves.

When I need to, I spend time with my family. They're set up with a nice home in a nice community. They don't want for anything. They have what they need to make them happy and that doesn't include me always hanging around like a bouncy dog constantly under their feet.

I'm like the sun and I let people into my orbit, but never for too long. It gets too crowded when you don't cut people loose and the chase is as much fun as the conquest.

I silo what I do and the people I spend time with. That way I can manage them; what they know and what parts of my life they have

access to. When someone threatens my status quo, boom, I do whatever is necessary to make sure that entity is permanently distanced. I never let anyone close to my family and there isn't or won't ever be anyone else that is essential in my life.

1-12 - - Stealth

"Do not be perceived; even within your enemy's eyesight." - - Birch Bentley

On Mondays the Executive Committee, technically just Al Perri and Donald Hightower, would meet at ten a.m. I wasn't a member of the Executive Committee, but Al brought me along occasionally because he liked to talk all week about the meetings. Being in on his Monday conversations with Hightower made me a better lunch and drinking buddy, when Al could tell me what he really thought.

Al would sit across from Hightower, who would sit behind his desk with never a loose paper to be seen anywhere. I sat on the sofa off to the side, speaking only when spoken to.

I made a point of being as invisible as possible. I would imagine myself as a Ninja, blending in and becoming part of the shape of the sofa. My arm would become the sofa's arm, my back the sofa's back. I wouldn't move a muscle. I never reacted to what was being discussed, so as to avoid even a glance in my direction.

There were missions I was on that would require me to be still for hours at a time. The slightest unnecessary move might give a position away which under the wrong circumstances could be life-threatening to me, or the entire team, jeopardizing the entire operation.

It was a little game I played with myself but it had a point. Hightower was as potentially explosive as a bottle of Nitro. I was determined not to do anything that would detonate him.

I've observed other people in these kinds of environments. They shake their leg, they click their pen, they check their phone for messages, they look at the pictures on the wall or become

interested in some distraction another person is causing; all while the key people are talking.

What would Hightower think if he looked over and saw me bouncing my leg up and down like I was trying to shake the building, or holding my phone in my face feverishly texting someone?

Compared to the stillness game I play in my meetings, these people are fools that demean themselves. They don't even belong in the same room with me; they belong in the clown car where they can drive to their next gig with the rest of the clowns. They might as well wear size eighteen red shoes with yellow sponge balls glued to the tips.

"Al, bring me up to date on the progress we're making with the ALH acquisition?" Hightower asked.

"Things are moving along. I just asked Birch here to expand the M&A team."

"Very good, Birch," Hightower said. His patronizing tone was similar to what my dad used after I brought home an A on a spelling test.

I looked at the way Hightower dressed. He had a penchant for grey suits, mostly on the darker side. He always wore a white shirt with monogrammed sleeves and breast pocket. His shoes were expensive; normally some shade of brown.

He had one shiny sharkskin grey suit. The funny thing was he always wore this pink tie with that sharkskin suit causing people who saw him regularly to realize that what he had on was an outfit. 'Mix it up a little, man; men don't wear outfits.'

"By the way, gentlemen, Cathy Black tendered her resignation Friday afternoon. A memo coming out shortly will name Geoff O'Reilly as temporary CFO until we find a permanent replacement."

By the way? *By the way?* Is that all Hightower had to say about it?

Cathy Black was a solid employee with decades of tenure. Corporations needed people like her to serve as the historians and be the keepers of the company culture. If bedrock like her were expendable, nobody was safe.

I avoided looking at Al Perri, afraid my expression would show the shock and anger I was feeling. Firing her was outrageous but nobody would dare say so to Hightower.

Regrettably, I stuck out my leg when I heard the news. It was more like a reflexive kick and it drew the attention of both Al and Hightower. They both looked at me, waiting to see if I was going to say anything.

I wanted to tell Hightower he was being a dick and say firing Cathy Black was craziness. That if the stock went back up $2.00 that week, or that month, there wasn't any graceful way for Cathy Black to be hired back? She would have been fired for nothing. This was a dumb, nonsensical decision, and there wasn't a thing anybody could do or say about it. So the freaking stock temporarily went down $2.00, it was a storm in a glass of water. Cathy Black would be another chapter in the legacy train wreck Hightower's pettiness cost the company.

Of course, I didn't say that and went back into Ninja mode on the sofa.

Al and Hightower discussed other matters and the meeting ended with a Hightower pep talk. He could hardly contain his giddiness over the prospects of the acquisition.

"Now listen, both of you. When the acquisition happens, events will move quickly. Our market cap right now is around a billion."

'Around a billion' was what I had said to Al in the limo.

"Investors will like this transaction," Hightower told us. "I believe our stock will jump from $50 to around $60. Let's all make this happen; sooner is better."

Hightower couldn't hide his exuberance for the transaction. If the stock price went to $60, Hightower's gains on his options would total about $2,500,000. The total shares he owned would yield him about $15,000,000.

The gain on my own stock options would total about $600,000.

Hightower's stock riches weren't small potatoes, but they were less than what most insurance chairman and CEO's received at the head of a company like Affluent Society. An undersized option package exposed his weak relationship with the Board of Directors.

The stock options were a replacement deal the board had approved in 2008, when the shares of Affluent Society tanked along with the stock market and the economy.

The one thing the stock options temporarily did was help shut Hightower up about a corporate jet. Hightower had been going after a corporate jet the way Al Perri chased women. The economic crash immediately ended any talk about private corporate aircraft.

Before conceding the corporate jet, Hightower had a near head-exploding experience over being turned down. The whole thing was just one more incident in a long history of contentious spats with the board.

That kind of arrogance, combined with his neglect of the board, is what would be his downfall. My instincts told me the board members had no fondness for Hightower, or Perri. The board would be my opening if I played my cards properly.

As we left the meeting, Hightower put his hand on my shoulder, a rare gesture on his part. Employees didn't touch Hightower, and he touched them only on the rarest occasions. You never saw him shaking anybody's hand. As company leaders go, he just wasn't that personable; and so his touch didn't reflect sociability; it represented jeopardy.

"Birch, I almost forgot to ask. You have that thing in Florida under control, right?"

40

The meeting was over and I had almost avoided having to talk about the one thing I didn't want to discuss. His question, combined with his hand on my shoulder, signaled to me how critical an issue he thought the trouble fermenting in Florida was.

The Florida issue was my biggest vulnerability. I had nothing to do with creating the issue but everything to do with fixing it. To make matters worse, it was being scrutinized more than normal because it could potentially adversely affect the merger discussions. It was akin to giving me a hand grenade with the pin missing.

"Not to worry, Mr. Hightower. I'm working closely with Jill Mahoney from legal on it."

"Good. We can't afford to have any due diligence hang ups once we get to a transaction point with ALH."

1-13 - - Cathy Black

22 years with the company and I'm let go like I was a temp brought in to help with the holiday rush. I gave everything to the company. I worked extra hours and weekends. I passed up vacations with the family. I watched the men around me doing less and earning more, and for the last eight years I've endured the verbal abuse of Donald Hightower.

What kind of mutant doesn't put the good of the company, and the people that work for it, into proper perspective? My husband's health isn't good, and one of our kids just bought a house and may need some help. My husband and I have plans on retiring to South Carolina in ten years. Where is that money going to come from now?

I'm devastated, humiliated, and angry. I've been punished unfairly. As soon as I get over my crying, I'm going to find an attorney and sue the ass off of Affluent Society. I may ask some of the other people who were unjustly let go to join me.

1-14 - - Fool's Folly

"All war is based on deception." - - Sun Tzu

I called Cathy Black at her home to offer my condolences.

"Cathy, this is Birch Bentley calling."

"Birch, this is unexpected. Thanks for calling."

"I just wanted to let you know that I appreciated the chance to work with you and offer to write a recommendation letter or help out in any way I can."

"Birch, that is so sweet of you. I may take you up on that offer sometime; in the meantime I'm just sorting things out."

"Understood, everybody around here is going to miss you. Is there anything I can do right now?"

"No, Birch, but thanks for the offer. Let's keep in touch."

I didn't know if it was true, but the rumor was that Cathy had been sleeping with one of the board members. If it was true, it wouldn't hurt to have Cathy as an ally if I needed her, and her board relationship, down the road.

"Where are we going for lunch?" Al asked when we left Hightower's office.

"Al, this is the day you told Trace he could come to lunch with us as a reward for a quarterly sales record."

Trace was our National Sales Manager.

"Shit," Al said. "I can't stand all that marketing bullshit. Tell him we have a two o'clock meeting so we don't have to sit there and discuss useless-ass sales crap."

Although extremely smart, Trace lacked the amount of acuity you would expect from someone in his position. In his mid-forties, he asked questions at lunch that demonstrated he wasn't going to be included in the inner circles of the boardroom anytime soon.

Maybe it was just me, but when I was with Trace he looked with his eyes, he listened with his ears, and he understood like a wall. As my Yiddish friends would say, 'the hat is fine, but the head is too small.'

I would have really liked to help Trace sort the realities out for him on a basis he would understand, but I knew he would fight the real explanation both intellectually and emotionally.

What somebody needed to do was sit down with Trace and explain the sham to him; show him an infographic that represented the truth of a situation. Of course, that wouldn't happen between sophisticated people at the top, because they understand the pretense without any discussion. If they don't, they don't belong at the top.

I tuned out their conversation and had an imaginary exchange in my head that would put across to Trace the information that he was missing.

Chairman says to the president: "I was reading the Wall Street Journal today, and I noticed that most of the chairman and presidents of four billion dollar companies were making significantly more pay than the chairmen and presidents of 2.5 billion dollar companies. Not only that, they all have their own company planes."

President: "Well, at our current growth rate, we'll be a four billion dollar company in 11 years."

Chairman: "I may be dead in 11 years. Or worse, shit for brains, I may be alive and my dick might not work. I want to be at $4 billion *now*, not in 11 years."

President: "How about if we start recruiting more agents and increase our new sales?"

Chairman: "You are really pathetic. I'm not interested in a program that's going to make the next chairman look like a genius. Figure out a way to get to $4 billion now or I'll find a president who can."

President: "I guess we could acquire another company with $1.5 billion in revenues if the price isn't too high."

Chairman: "Too high! You idiot! You're talking like you're spending your own money. Let me say this one more time, slowly. I'm chairman of a $2.5 billion company. I want to increase company revenues to $4 billion because I'll not only get a lot more money from this job, but I can demand a lot more at my next job and maybe, just maybe, get more sex at home. Now are you going to help me, or do I need another president?"

President: "No worries, I'll find the other $1.5 billion in revenue."

Chairman: "Good, now get your sorry ass up out of that chair and out of my office before I decide to look for another president anyhow."

Trace might get that if the con was ever articulated out loud, but the ruse is buried in secrecy and not mentioned even in private. There is no need to, because the players who matter grasp the unspoken actuality.

If you didn't understand, you didn't get to play the game at that level.

If I were Trace's Dad, or mentor, I might have taken him aside later and clarified what was happening and why. Since I wasn't, Trace was going to have to figure things out for himself - if he ever does.

Not to mention that to wizen Trace up would be breaking the code. You don't go around revealing what's going on with the insiders if you want to remain an insider. People on the inside know how to keep their mouths shut.

Important and powerful people have their boundaries set tight, especially in the presence of a fool, and shun someone who doesn't have the discipline or the common sense to shut up.

1-15 - - Concealment & Deception

"I have two secret weapons: concealment and deception." - - Birch Bentley

My first date with Jennifer was for dinner at 7:00; about as early as I can normally get away with. I liked to eat early, but I also liked to give myself as much time after dinner for the pursuit of other possibilities. I didn't want the hour dictating how the evening was going to end.

Jennifer was tall with a baby smooth complexion. Her green eyes contrasted with the orangey-red lipstick she was wearing. Her eyebrows were still natural and not over-plucked. Her nose was close to classic, and she had the slightest of chin dimples that you had to be near to notice. Made up for our date, she could have been described as flawless.

She possessed what Al Perri referred to as the three B's: Beauty, Body, and Brains.

There was a fourth B we sometimes discussed, bank account, but only if we thought net worth might be eight figures or more. A woman's finances were a non-issue with me, although marrying for money isn't a bad strategy for getting in if you have no other options.

'No wealth? Then marry wealth.' In business they teach you all the time to bridge your weaknesses through others. You can be rich in less than a year if you have the smarts to marry the right woman and are willing to live with the consequences; although that would be too big a price for me to pay.

If you look in any history book, you'll find people have been marrying for fortune and position since the beginning of time. For whatever reason it isn't held in fashion by the majority of Americans now even though it may be the fastest, simplest, and easiest way to riches. It's simple, marry up.

I had an aunt and uncle back in California who used to joke all the time that their Plan B was to get divorced and each marry somebody well off. They're still together and doing extremely well in real estate.

This uncle was influential in my life. He gave me a book entitled "Think And Grow Rich" by Napoleon Hill, and told me to read it several times until the message was part of my core. I still read my highlights once a year, although I've discovered new books that moved to top spot on my most important books list.

'The Art Of War by Sun Tzu – 200 Quotes' and 'The Prince, by Niccolò Machiavelli – 200 Quotes,' both summaries by Roth Stanton, were now my compass.

"Jennifer, you look great! I hope we bump into somebody important I know so they can be impressed. "

"Are those for me?" Jennifer asked as she looked at the flower arrangement I was holding.

"Yes, I saw how beautiful they looked and thought you might enjoy them."

Bringing Jennifer flowers was a little corny but she was the kind of girl that would appreciate the gesture. The effort told her I thought she was special and I was focused on my evening with her. I was sure the small act separated me from the other first-date wags she'd been out with. As scarce as money was growing up, my parents never went to anyone's house without some type of thoughtful gift or tribute, small as it might be.

"That is *so* thoughtful, Birch. Thank you."

Someone even more beautiful than Jennifer walked into the room wearing a tank top and a pair of tight short shorts. The way she filled out her tank top didn't leave you wondering if she was wearing a bra.

"Birch, this is my roommate, Brenda. Brenda, this is Birch."

"Hello." I said as I reached to shake Brenda's hand.

I hoped I wasn't drooling. I wanted to stare at the magnificent pair of breasts in front of me, but I knew what a gigantic mistake that would be - speaking of gigantic.

With every bit of willpower I had, I turned toward Jennifer.

"You look breathtaking, and the dress is perfect for where we're going! We have reservations at Virtuoso's in Greenwich Village at 7:30."

Virtuoso's was one of those trendy Manhattan restaurants with a classic bar, great food presentation with those special little touches, and fairly high prices - the kind of place sure to meet Jennifer's expectations. You know ahead of time you're going to have to wait for a table, even with reservations. We gave our name to the hostess and went into the bar area for some wine.

"Tell me a little about the business you're in, Jennifer."

"It's incentive travel," she replied. "There are a lot of people already making a good buck whose attention you can't get anymore with just extra money - but tack on a free exotic trip full of food, fun, adventure, and - forgive me - the possibility they may get lucky," she blushed, "and they will bust their butts to qualify. Our company caters to the companies that sponsor those kinds of trips."

The dinner was going great, which is exactly what I'd expected. She was gorgeous, intelligent, and great fun. I was a reasonably attractive man: in shape, successful in my career, thoughtful and unselfish in my approach if not my motives. I was clued in what to do or not to do; for example, I was always careful not to use my robot or pirate voice on a first date. Not the best way to make a good first impression.

Want to have a second date? Don't growl "Aarrrghhhh" in your pirate's voice or order your appetizer in your robot voice on the first.

The whole time I'm sitting there I'm thinking about Brenda back at the apartment by herself in her tank top and short shorts. How is it that she doesn't have a date on a Saturday night?

The conversation with Jennifer was easy and she laughed a lot. Her smile was genuine and pure. The talk turned to relationships, as first date dinner conversations always do sooner or later.

"Have you ever been married?" Jennifer asked me.

"No," I said, "I came close once, but marriage didn't happen. I've been kind of waiting until I find the right one. What about you?"

I guessed Jennifer's answer would be no, because Jennifer was at least 10 years younger than me and she was career focused. This was perfect as far as I was concerned. I didn't get the impression that she had that fear her biological clock was ticking that women seem to get some time around the age of 30.

Not that I blamed women, didn't understand their concern, or wasn't sympathetic to their situation; I was. It's just I didn't want to be the solution to their issue, at least not right then. I would rather seek out women who weren't unduly anxious about their marital status.

The whole issue is unfair, so I just attempt to make it is as fair as I can and consider where the other person is in their life.

"No, I've never been married either, Birch; someday, I suppose. Right now I'm focused on my career and whatever quality time I can manage. Quality time with someone whose company I really enjoy is what matters to me. If I can't be spending quality time with someone special, I would really just prefer to stay home."

I knew exactly what she meant because I felt the same way myself. The difference is that my definition of quality time included all the same things a girl like Jennifer did, but didn't stop with the kind of list a girl like Jennifer would come up with.

Having said that, regard for other people's viewpoint entails respect for what they think and to consider how women feel about relationships and commitment, even if I didn't feel compelled to agreeing with their perspective myself. I had a simple and workable guideline – 'don't mislead or hurt anyone.'

Would someone steal my heart and lasso me in someday? Sure; surrender just wasn't likely to be that day.

This first date with Jennifer was amazing and I enjoyed her company. There was an attraction that told me she could be a game changer even though I wasn't looking for the game to change.

After dinner we went to a wine bar and talked until about eleven. When we left to take Jennifer home I still had no real idea if she was going to invite me up for a nightcap, or more.

As much as I liked Jennifer I wondered if it would be bad form to ask Brenda out. There must be a way to work that out without looking like a complete jerk. It's incredible how the mind can hold two conflicting thoughts at the same time.

1-16 - - Jennifer Sable

I've been waiting a long time to meet someone like Birch.

He is handsome, smart, successful, funny, and most importantly, he is nice. His mother raised him right and you don't find that much anymore.

Now that I've met a man that I could spend the rest of my life with it's a bit thorny. If I do anything that makes him feel rushed, he's the kind of man that will back off - but if I don't press things he may just fade away or be attracted by a shiny new object.

I should be everything Birch wants in a woman as well. The trouble is that society is all disjointed today. Too many mixed messages, and people have lost sight of what's really important.

If Birch is as smart as I think he is he will come to realize that he should marry me and be brilliantly happy raising a family and making a life together.

All I can do is hope that he figures that out for himself.

1-17 - - Brenda

I don't know how Jennifer always ends up finding these perfect guys. The thing that annoys me the most is she doesn't know what to do once she's attracted them.

Get me out on a date with them and I'll have their head spinning and their world turned upside down. That's what men are looking for.

I could feed off her table scraps when it comes to men, but I don't want to wreck our relationship. I've got too sweet a deal with our apartment and it's just too hard to find decent, affordable digs in a place like New York.

2) Florida Fiasco

2-1 - - Trouble Brewing

"The best way to escape from a problem is to solve it."-
- Brendan Francis

On Monday morning I took a call from Jill Mahoney who headed up our legal department.

"Birch, I received some additional correspondence from the Florida Department of Insurance," she began.

"How serious do you think this is, Jill? The timing is really not the greatest right now. Upstairs is getting restless over this whole situation."

"If the regulators draw a target on our backs, we're dead meat. The safest thing here is to stay under the radar if possible."

Anything that might negatively affect the deal with ALH would have caused Hightower to go into a rage with his face turning the color of a red pepper.

"Jill, give me your best recommendations in writing. If necessary I'll go down to Florida to meet with the regulators. Also, list anyone we know through our Political Action Committee who could help if needed."

My job was to resolve this issue and not let Hightower or Perri get their hands dirty with the details.

A properly established chain of communication ensured that no one ever knew what the CEO thought or said about a potentially hot issue. Jill was talking directly to me to separate Hightower and Perri from direct contact with the problem.

Jill talked to me, I talked to Al, and I assume Al talked to Hightower. Under this scenario, by design; Jill had no definite insight about what Al or Hightower thought, and I had no clue about Hightower's thinking.

What didn't happen under this structure was that neither Jill, me, or anybody else would ever hear Hightower say "Screw the attorney general and screw the policy owners until after ALH agrees to the merger. The merger takes precedence over everything else. Has everybody got it?"

The inaccurate perception for public consumption is that a CEO will always make decisions based on the best interest of the policy owners. What an absurdity. Hightower didn't care about the policy owners; he cared about the acquisition and how much his stock would be worth.

Business chronicles are filled with stories of insiders making bad deals for the shareholders because the personal deals for themselves in the transaction were overly generous. Trying to pass laws to prevent this type of greed and self-dealing is pointless because you can never prove it, even though it is there plain as day for everyone to see.

I went to my iPad and looked at the list of options I had created for myself, specifically for resolving the Florida complication. I had a practice of writing my thoughts and ideas on my personal iPad and e-mailing them to my private Gmail account.

I knew any e-mails I sent using the company platform would be retained indefinitely. I didn't want any personal or sensitive data circulating through the company tech systems where an IT person could retrieve them at some later time, with or without my consent.

I kept lists of ideas for everything on my iPad. Many of them were far out in left field, but they served to keep me thinking outside of the box. On several occasions, something I'd dismissed as completely foolish actually led to a workable idea.

I had two options for dealing with the Florida regulatory investigation: solve the problem in a way that settled the matter immediately and decisively, or let the concern lie and hope no trouble followed.

The glitch with the latter course was that if I let things lie and a snag popped up to spoil the merger, I'd have some explaining to do.

Set in those terms, I had to make the problem go away permanently. Doing anything else might be the basis for a career-ending catastrophe.

Managing these kinds of issues were what made me worth my middle-six figure salary.

2-2 - - Lana Lang

"The only way to get rid of temptation is to yield to it."
- - Oscar Wilde, The Picture of Dorian Gray

My cell phone rang and the caller I.D. said LL. I use initials to save my contacts on my cell phone because you never know who is looking at your phone. I knew it was Lana Lang.

"Hello Lana, how are you?"

"Birch, I'm fine and I'm sorry we haven't been in contact, I've been out of the country. What has it been, almost two weeks, right?"

I told myself to just be cool, like nobody had ever said anything to you,

"I've been busy myself. Where did you go?"

Shit, why did I ask her that question? It's the exact question I would have asked if I was working with Miller.

"Back to Paris, banking stuff. Are we going to get together again?"

Lana asked this in a manner that said she already knew the answer would be yes.

I'd been thinking for two weeks about what I would say when she called and I was still stuck for an answer.

"What did you have in mind?"

"I'm having dinner with my boss on Saturday. Why don't you join us?"

The boss that has something to do with missing people? I don't think so.

"I'm sorry, but I know I'm busy on Saturday." Trying to sound regretful but not too much.

"Then why don't you come over on Sunday and watch the Giants on my big screen T.V. with me? I'll get some pizza and chips and we'll break open a special bottle of wine I've been saving."

Lana Lang should have been named Lana Luscious. She was put together as well as a person can be. Her ass moved liked it had its own motor. I should go over there, have sex with her, and then tell her I felt guilty because I had started seeing someone. That would seem like what a normal guy would do without raising any suspicion. Blowing her off after the electricity we had generated is what would look strange.

"Count me in. I'll be there in time for the kickoff."

2-3 - - CEO Greed

"If a man does not keep pace with his companions, perhaps it is because he hears a different drummer. Let him step to the music which he hears, however measured and far away." - - Henry David Thoreau (1817 - 1862) from Walden

"Birch, let's go. Lunch is at Augustino's today. I want to dine upscale because I'm inspired by what I read in the Boston Globe this morning."

Augustino's was located between Soho and Tribeca. Al liked to point out that the women who came in were mostly beautiful. Even if they weren't stunning, they maximized everything they did have with expensive clothes and perfect makeup. Augustino's had an unwritten rule: No style, no service — only beautiful people allowed.

Al normally liked this restaurant for the women it attracted but right then he had his mind on other things; namely, money.

"Did you see this report in the Boston Globe?" Al asked me.

"No, I haven't."

The article profiled the president of a large property and casualty company headquartered in Boston. The president had raked in an average income of nearly $50 million per year for the three years before he retired.

"Al, that's serious money, but it's nothing like that guy in California who left his health insurance company with over a billion dollars in his pocket. And what about that guy at the stock exchange, how much did he pay himself — $400 million or something like that?"

"Birch, I'm telling you it's unbelievable, unbelievable. Makes me look like a piker. Hightower is going to shit his pants when he reads this today, and I'm telling you, he wants a shot at that kind

of money. He'll never let ALH go, no matter what the cost, because the acquisition is his opportunity to make more money than someone like you could ever even imagine: $50 million dollars a year for three straight years, this guy made."

I wondered why Al thought I couldn't imagine making that much money.

"Listen, Birch, you and I can make that kind of money too," Al continued - contradicting what he had just said about me less than a minute ago.

"We have to work together and protect one another. I mean, when the CEO moves out, I'm going to go right up to his level, and you'll go up a notch with me. There's only one way to get into that inner circle, Birch, and that's for somebody to take you in. You can be the smartest mother in the world, and the politics and bullshit will still keep you out. But I'll get you in."

I'd seen Al work over so many people that his con was obvious to me. I knew for a fact that Al had never cared about another person's welfare in his entire life.

What Al meant was he would bring me in with him *if* he thought that helped him. On the other hand, if my involvement didn't help, Al would dismiss me and say, "well, that's the way the cookie crumbles."

Al would sell me out in a minute. I knew he would, and he knew he would.

What I wasn't sure of is whether he knew I knew, or whether he thought I was buying into his load of crap.

Still he was right in one respect. If I wanted to get on the inside, one of my best options would be for Al to get on the inside first and hold the door open for me. Al's nature made this a big gamble; there was a fifty-fifty chance he would pull a Lucy and yank the football just when my turn to kick had arrived.

Having Al walk me in wasn't my only option. The safer play would be to take Hightower and Perri out, organizationally speaking, if I could figure out how to do it.

"And remember, Birch, everyone makes a bundle at the top. Hell, right before I left the office I looked on Google. The average person at the top of an S&P-listed life insurance company earned $4.8 million. I'm surprised Hightower isn't on my back about this every day. He isn't even close to the average level."

I knew Hightower made around $3.5 million from the SEC filings we did each year, and Al wasn't that far behind him at $2.9 million. But neither of them were at benchmark levels for a company the size of Affluent Society; a fact that would eat away at the guts of greedy S.O.B.'s like Hightower and Perri.

They had money out the wazoo, but they still wanted to take, take, and take some more. They would take as much as they could for as long as they could; until somebody stopped them.

2-4 - - Unanticipated Warmth

"A pleasure unexpected is the sweetest of all." - - Birch Bentley

I was reaching the point in my relationship with Jennifer where I would prefer to entertain her than go out with Al; a dangerous relationship stage. We were often talking on the phone two or three times a day and seeing each other twice a week.

My biggest problem with Jennifer is that I had mentally planted a "Brenda trigger" in my subconscious that caused me to think about Brenda more than I should have been.

On the phone with Jennifer in the afternoon I told her where Al and I would be that night and asked her to show up and act surprised to see me.

+++

"Wow, Jennifer, you look stunning tonight."

Jennifer looked amazing. Her hair was perfect, her makeup was perfect, her body was perfect and she was dressed in a sleek body-hugging dress that clung to her tightly in the right places and showed off her obvious assets. In their twenties, women's bodies can be amazing.

I was tempted to take her over and show her off to Al who was engrossed in a conversation with a new friend, but I knew that would be a mistake.

"Jennifer, can you wait here for a minute, I want to close out my tab."

I was going to tell Al I was leaving but he was grooving on his latest conquest so I just left.

"Ready?" I asked Jennifer.

We got into a cab and went to a much quieter place just a few blocks away.

"Jennifer, I feel like I was just rescued by an angel,"

"Thanks, getting all dressed up once in a while does feel good."

"You'd turn heads anywhere you went looking like that, but enough with the compliments. Tell me everything that has happened to you since we last got together and I want you to go into great detail. Don't leave out a thing."

The truth is I loved looking at the woman I was out with. I noticed every nuance, how they laughed, how they held their head when they were talking about certain subjects. Did they like to talk about their job, their family, their old relationships? I loved every second from the first word to the last; and the entire time I was thinking about how exciting and wonderful the ending would be when this angelic creature God created surrendered her body to me and I made her shudder in ecstasy.

"Birch, look, I'm attracted to you, but I'm not going to sleep with someone this soon in a relationship."

This soon? It had already been about three weeks. I was certain that if I'd been dating Brenda, our clothes would have been off two weeks ago. The best ones are always the hardest to get into bed.

Hanging on into the relationship this long without sex was a clue I'd have to be careful about my feelings toward Jennifer; they could easily get out of control.

2-5 - - Florida On My Mind

"Shallow men believe in luck or in circumstance. Strong men believe in cause and effect." - - Ralph Waldo Emerson

It's a funny thing about New Yorkers. They all insisted they loved the city and yet I never met one that didn't dream of escaping to Miami.

I needed to go to Florida personally to handle several aspects of my plan to deal with the potential regulatory issues and terminate the people involved. The serendipity of this was that Sandy Lockheart in compliance was the best person in the organization to help facilitate my meetings with the regulators.

"Sandy, this is Birch Bentley. Can you tell me who it is you deal with at the Department of Insurance in Florida?"

"Several people, Birch, depending on what it is. Can I be of help with anything?"

"I need to go to Florida on some other matters, and I want to meet with the most Senior Insurance Department people I can while I'm there. Do you think you could arrange that?"

"I can try; when did you have in mind?"

"Week after next and if your schedule is clear, I would like you to plan to go along as well. You can help provide the introductions and smooth out the conversation with the insurance department people. Would that be O.K.?"

"I don't see why not. I'll check with my mother tonight to see if she can watch the children just to make sure there are no family obligations. Can I let you know definitely tomorrow? I'm recently divorced so being a single parent is making travel more difficult."

"Thanks, Sandy, just let me know when you have an answer."

Sandy sent me an e-mail that said her schedule was clear and I replied and asked her if we could meet near the end of the day to review the issues. My assistant Sean arranged the meeting for 4:30 p.m. in my office.

Sandy was right on time for our 4:30 meeting.

My office was large enough to hold a round conference table for four people. I preferred to sit at the table rather than behind my desk when working with someone. This was especially true when working with someone like Sandy. She wore fairly short skirts, and with legs like hers, who could blame her if she liked to show them off a little bit?

Tremendous self-discipline was called for not to stare at her legs. She had great physical energy with constant motion resulting in a behavior of scooting her chair out and sitting squarely facing me to make a point. The more points she made, the higher her skirt was getting and the more distracting her legs became.

There wasn't the slightest indication that she was even aware of this, but I was certain she would have to be aware of her impact on a man in this situation.

"Birch, here's the organization chart of the Florida Insurance Department."

I couldn't focus at all on what she was saying. I was too busy with my man fantasy that she was some kind of nymphomaniac who wanted me.

As ridiculous as Sandy being a raving nympho, was for someone of her intellect and life experience to not be mindful of her tease and the effect on me.

As I went back to my desk to take a telephone call, Sandy stood up for no apparent reason, keeping her elbows on the table and without taking her eyes off the paperwork she was inspecting. She was bent over the table seemingly completely focused on the work, but her body was saying something wholly different. The arch of her back was pulling up her dress so that I could see a great deal of her legs. From the right angle, I would probably be able to say *"Helloooo, panties."*

As much as I was tempted, I couldn't afford to be wrong there in my office. At work I had no way of determining Sandy's motivation: was she sending me a signal, did she just like to show off her body, was she setting some kind of trap?

Maybe she just had too much energy and had to move around a lot. Men would love to have the insight to know how women think in those kinds of situations, but no one knows how a woman thinks and especially not a man.

I always took the view that women feel as much as they think, but even that knowledge didn't keep me out of trouble all the time. I often thought that being in touch with their emotions gives women an advantage over men in several ways.

After a few minutes Sandy sat back down, but I was about to explode. The sensation was the same teen experience I'd had back in high school, sitting in class fantasizing about frenching the World Affairs teacher after school.

"Sandy, why don't you finish this tomorrow and send everything up to me?"

Before I have an accident in my pants, or possibly in yours, right here in my office.

"Anything you say, Mr. Bentley. Is that all for now?"

"Yes, I have another call to make and another appointment."

2-6 - - Hatchet Man

"If you wish to be perfect, go, sell your possessions, and give the money to the poor, and you will have treasure in heaven; then come, follow me." When the young man heard this word, he went away grieving, for he had many possessions." Matthew 19:21

"Sean, I need you to get Vince Carter on the telephone for me."

I was referring to the Manager of our Orlando Life Insurance Office. Vince Carter was the General Agent in Florida who had hired an agent from another company, an agent who now was named as part of the investigation by the Florida Insurance Department and Attorney General's office.

I knew what I had to do and I didn't like that I had to do it. Most likely the people I was going to take down were decent folks who would have their lives seriously disrupted, possibly permanently. But this is why I was getting paid the big bucks: to do what had to be done when it was needed. What was required right then was for me to take on the role of hatchet man.

The irony of this struck me. I was the hatchet man, doing the dirty work to protect greedy rat bastards like Al Perri and Donald Hightower so they could get even richer. When you're a kid you never say you want to be a hatchet man when you grow up.

I knew our agent; Brad Bishop, was going to be fired. If I refused to fire him and something went wrong with the investigation, I would be going next. There was no ethics or morality involved, just a fact: Brad Bishop was going to be fired.

My study of 'The Art Of War' by Sun Tzu taught me that leaders have been getting other people to do their dirty work for at least 2,500 years. The king gives the orders to his general, who gives the orders to his officers.

The king, or the Chairman in my case, had told his general, Al Perri to get the Florida situation handled, and Al gave his order to his officer, me, and now I was going to Florida to eliminate Brad Bishop and his supervisor Vince Carter.

"Vince, this is Birch Bentley from Affluent Society here in New York. How are you doing down there today?"

"Just great, Mr. Bentley."

"How's the weather down there, Vince?" I asked. "Because I'm going to be down in Florida week after next. I have to do some compliance work. I'll be glad to get out of this New York snow and cold."

I was sure he knew I wasn't calling to ask about the weather.

"It's actually nice this time of year; in the 70's most days."

"That's great Vince, there's another matter. Tell me a little from your perspective about that agent we hired from SSL. What's his name?"

I had Brad Bishop's complete file in front of me.

"His name is Brad Bishop, Mr. Bentley; he came to us from SSL about 18 months ago. Set a State of Florida record for the most premium produced in an agent's first 12 months with the company."

"Well, what's all this about replacement trouble?"

I knew exactly what the trouble was.

"Mr. Bentley, Brad is as honest as they come. All this fuss, and the only thing Brad has ever done is to help people improve their financial situation by using the cash value in an older policy to fund a newer policy with higher interest rates and a larger face amount."

The poor son-of-a-bitch. Vince, like Brad, was gone anyhow, but the more he defended Brad Bishop, the more he looked like part of the collusion. Unfair, but the policy twisting did happen on his watch.

I would have liked to help him and Brad, but I was powerless to help. Worse, I was playing the character of executioner. All this

was just a charade until I could go down there and properly terminate the both of them.

"In your opinion, Vince, was there full disclosure at the time of sale?"

"Mr. Bentley, the necessary documentation exists, but you know how confusing insurance is for most people. Excuse my language, but the damn Attorney General down here and some trouble-maker lawyers are painting a picture of the big bad insurance company taking advantage of the little old defenseless policy owner. Frankly, the whole thing burns my ass something fierce."

"Don't worry, Vince; the full resources of Affluent Society Insurance are available to make sure nobody gets bulldozed here. Now when I get to Florida, I want to meet with you and Brad; and I want you to have all the documentation available for me to look at. Can you do that?"

"Yes, Mr. Bentley, I can." Carter sounded relieved.

"Good, nobody's going to roll-over and lay down at Affluent Society just because there are some dogs barking. I'll be seeing you soon."

I thought about another of my favorite quotes: 'The dogs bark and the train rolls on.'

Sean was in my office and had been listening in on my end of the conversation.

"You're going down to Florida to fire them, right, Birch?"

"Right, Sean."

"Why not just terminate them over the phone?"

"Because we're in the middle of a merger and the Florida Insurance Department is involved. This has to be done right. I'm personally going to Florida to terminate Brad Bishop and Vince Carter and tipping them off makes no sense because the decision

is final. Too much information in advance would just make the situation messier than it has to be."

"Does anyone care that they may be getting shafted?" Sean frowned.

"That misses the point, Sean."

"Which is?"

"That Affluent Society isn't going to take on the Attorney General of Florida and a vicious group of shyster fee-hounds to save Vince's and Brad's butts. Not with the ALH Life deal pending. I hate the process but I'm powerless to change it. Here's what you have to understand, Sean. Business is complicated, but no matter what, the beast must survive. There are no innocents here; we all show up to serve the beast."

"The beast being Affluent Society?"

"Precisely."

"Birch, if you ever need to fire me don't play any games with me; just tell me straight out."

"Sean, I'm nothing here but the messenger boy doing what he is told; and playing the game the way winners play. We may not like the rules but that's the way life is. I gave up trying to be a Boy Scout a long time ago."

"Not reassuring, Birch, and not a nice game."

"It's not meant to be, Sean, so put your big boy pants when you come to work in the morning and be ready for the rough and tumble of business or be prepared to have your lunch eaten by others. We're not here to make friends."

"You know, Sean; you've never asked me about this rubber alligator on my credenza?"

Sean shrugged. "I overheard you tell somebody one time it was to remind you that you were going to retire in Florida one day."

"That's what I tell people, Sean, but it's only half the story. It's pretty real looking for rubber, don't you think?"

"Yes."

"Look at it closely, Sean. Does the gator look like it's smiling to you?"

"Actually, Birch, it does sort of look like it has a grin on its face."

"If you pay attention, Sean, all alligators look that way when they're poised waiting for their next meal. They are very still, and they smile because they are certain they are going to eat. We can learn a lesson from the alligators. Do you know what it is?"

"No, tell me, Birch."

"Lay there quietly beneath the surface with your eyes open and when you see your prey, devour it mercilessly. And don't forget; while you're waiting, *smile*."

2-7 - - Sean

I don't think there's anyone that has a better perspective of Birch Bentley than I do.

He has no male friends that I know of.

I never hear him refer to family except occasionally I hear him mention something about his mother. I know his father passed away several years ago; Birch had come close to choking up the two times he mentioned him to me.

He's a mystery to most people but not to me. A genuine nice guy who wouldn't hurt anybody; except when he has to – which seems to be frequently.

He's always on his iPad doing what I think is strategizing, because sometimes I'll walk into his office when he's working on it and he'll float some really outlandish idea to see what I think about it.

He says he doesn't suck up to Al Perri but I don't know what else you'd call it. He practically jumps out of his chair and goes racing up to Al's office when he calls, no matter what else he's in the middle of.

I'll say this about him. He's self-disciplined like he went to West Point or somewhere, although I know he didn't. He mentions the military occasionally and sometimes I wonder if he ever had Special Forces training. His core value is self-improvement but I hate all his quotes and metaphors. He should really stop sharing those with everybody.

Girls love him, although I think they're somewhat deceived by that nice-guy persona that he tries to make everyone swallow. He always has two or three that he's seeing at any given time.

From a distance he seems like that guy that guys want to be and girls just want, but if they knew him up close they wouldn't be that eager. He has flaws, just like the rest of us.

2-8 - - False Values

Be extremely subtle, even to the point of formlessness. Be extremely mysterious, even to the point of soundlessness. Thereby you can be the director of the opponent's fate. - - Sun Tzu

Al always had the same information I had, probably more, but he would portray himself as completely in the dark and question me for every detail and response I could offer. He had a gift of doing this while revealing nothing of how he felt on an issue.

"Birch, can you come over to my office? I need an update on the situation in Florida."

Al was my biggest time waster. He would have me come into his office and spend hours talking about the same things or sometimes nothing at all, just a drifting conversation. We would repeat conversations we'd already had, sentence by sentence. He would take a telephone call and make me sit there while he

chatted with whomever. If I made a move like I was going to leave he would motion for me to sit back down in the chair.

Al's behavior was controlling, which was one of the few things I didn't handle well. I would bring my iPad in, but only look at it if he was on the phone. He did not extend me the same courtesy. Al would reads e-mails, type replies, take and make telephone calls, talk to his assistant, have meetings with whomever, all while I'm sitting in front of him like I was one of the chairs; just another piece of the office décor.

My solace was in knowing there would come a time when I would turn on him, like the lion that finally decides to turn on his trainer, and maul him into pieces. I didn't realize then how fast the day that one of us would be mauled was approaching.

"Al, here's the deal. I'm going to Florida and I'll be terminating the agent, Brad Bishop, and his superior, Vince Carter. That should cut the accountability at that level and not leave any line back to Affluent Society Insurance."

"Then, I'm going to meet with some people from the Florida Department of Insurance and make sure we're safe from anything else. I also have Jill Mahoney in legal working right now with our political action committee determining the feasibility of a contribution to the Insurance Commissioner's campaign fund. When I get back, I expect to have the matter over and dealt with."

Al looked at me with mock concern on his face.

"O.K. Birch, that sounds like a good plan. I hate to hang the two gentlemen out to dry like that, but if you think that's the best thing to do, we'll support you. You're sure they were caught up in this twisting thing and all that?"

What a crock. Al would have the two so called 'gentlemen' publicly executed if he thought capital punishment was needed to save the ALH deal. Al loved that he could feign compassion for the two lives that were about to be ruined while his hands remained clean.

"Just so you know, Birch, the Chairman keeps asking me about this whole affair and why the matter hasn't been handled yet."

"We're firing two people Al; we have to proceed by the book in a legal manner that isn't going to cause a ruckus. Don't worry; I've got this thing managed."

At least I thought I did.

2-9 - - Facade

"A façade as thin as a tissue does not conceal." - - Birch Bentley

On Sunday I arrived at Lana's about 12:30. I liked watching football but I had a different type of scoring on my mind. When Lana opened the door I went in and was immediately bummed out. She had company.

"Birch, come in, there's somebody I want you to meet" Lana said in an outside voice.

"Don't worry, they won't be staying long," she whispered as I walked from the hallway into her apartment.

As we went into her living room she resumed talking in a normal volume.

"Birch, I was out to dinner with my boss and some business associates last night like I said I would be, and when I told them about you and said you would be coming over today, they wanted to come and meet you."

She invites me over to watch a football game and tells me her boss wants to meet me? What the hell is so special about me except that they want something?

There was Lana's boss, sitting on the sofa, drinking the wine that Lana and I were supposed to be sharing, by ourselves.

"Birch, this is Arina. Arina, this is Birch."

I looked at Arina who was an older, very well maintained version of Lana.

"This is Yuri who also works for our company," Lana continued.

Arina spoke first.

"Birch, I'm so pleased to meet you. Lana has told me so much about you."

I should have gotten the hell out of there but Lana was hot, and so was Arina. Yuri was older, probably in his early fifties, but he was one of those guys that would be doing twenty-something's well into his sixties. I found myself drawn in.

"What can I get you to drink, Birch?" Lana asked me.

"I'll have whatever wine everybody is drinking. I brought a bottle of Chateau Montelena Estate Cabernet Sauvignon, 2010, to share as well."

This was a great bottle of wine. People that know wine always say the vintage, type, and year of the wine they brought. A good bottle of wine should be 'introduced,' announced with 'respect.'

I sat down and made small talk and waited to see what was going to happen. It didn't take that long for Yuri to start his probe.

"What exactly do you do at Affluent Society, Birch? Lana tells me you are one of the top people."

"Well, there are a lot of top people. I'm a senior vice president."

"Interesting, have you been the senior vice president long?"

"Not really, just a few months."

"What did you do for them before that?"

"I was in their fast start program so I moved around a lot spending time in various departments, but my background is law. I

started with the company out of law school in the compliance department."

"We spend a lot of time at our bank on compliance issues. Helping people manage their assets becomes harder and harder every day."

"I understand."

"You know, we might be able to be of help to each other, Birch. I'm sure your company sells annuities, right?"

"Yes, we do a lot of business with annuities."

"We have a lot of clients that want to move their money out of their own currency and into dollars. They think annuities from a U.S. company are a good way to go."

"I can understand why people would feel that way."

"Let's not talk too much business today, Birch, why don't you come by our bank sometime and we can discuss it."

"That sounds like a good idea, Yuri."

You know what else sounds like a good idea? For you and Arina to stop drinking all the wine and get your butts off Lana's chairs and out the door so Lana and I can take care of our business.

2-10 - - Shadowing

"Being in the company of someone under surveillance casts a spotlight upon oneself." - - Birch Bentley

On Monday morning I got a call from my favorite FBI agent.

"Birch, this is Special Agent Miller."

"Do you have to say Special Agent Miller every time you identify yourself?"

71

"Yes and it's no problem. Hey, how about those Giants yesterday? I love it when they beat up on the Eagles."

"I didn't see that much of the game."

"Too bad, were you occupied?"

"Did you call me up to play games with me?"

"No, I called you up because I was worried about you."

"Why would you be worried about me?"

"I heard you were moving up the food chain yesterday. You not only met Lana's boss, Arina, but you met Yuri as well."

"Are you watching me?"

"No, we're watching them."

"I went there to tell Lana I was seeing somebody else and break it off with her."

"How did she take the news?"

"Actually, I never got to tell her."

"How inconvenient."

"Very."

"Did you find anything out I might be interested in?"

I found out a lot. I already knew what the game was from talking with Yuri for five minutes. I could already speculate on the kind of illegal schemes the Russians could be running, but I wasn't going to tell Miller that.

"Not really."

"Well, let's stay in touch. Watch yourself, these people are dangerous. Their only interest in you is to use your position at Affluent Society.

"Thanks for the warning."

"Stay well."

2-11 - - Double Tequila

"Gonna make you lose your fight,
Gonna get you drunk tonight,
Gonna set your emo right!"
- - Birch Bentley

On Tuesday Sandy and I left La Guardia for Florida on the 8:10 a.m. direct flight. With a little luck I'd be sun-tanning right after lunch, and with a *lot* of luck doing something a lot more exciting than sun-tanning after that.

Our meeting with Vince and Brad Bishop was set for 9:30 a.m. the next morning and the insurance department representatives were scheduled after that for lunch.

I made sure the reservations were for an early morning flight and used some of my points to upgrade Sandy to first-class.

When we arrived in Orlando, we caught a cab to the Peabody which is a fabulous hotel. When you roll up to the front you feel like more than you've arrived at the hotel, you feel like you've arrived at life. The complex is massive and the inside shouts luxury and excess everywhere you look.

We may not all be able to own a home that resembles something from 'Lifestyles of the Rich and Famous', but we can rent that kind of experience for less than $300.00 a night.

We checked in, and I asked Sandy if she wanted to have lunch in the restaurant or poolside.

"How about poolside, you said you wanted to work on your tan?"

"Great, I'll be down there almost immediately. Come on down whenever."

I went to my room, hung up my clothes, and put on my swimsuit. I took a condom out of my travel bag without unpacking the rest of my gear, grabbed my sun tan lotion, iPhone and Kindle, and was out the door. I took two steps and decided to go back in my room and get a second condom.

At the entrance to the pool I arranged for a private cabana to be charged to my room and was led to a small tent canopy that opened on the side facing the pool.

Under the canopy was some expensive patio furniture, a lounge bed for two, and some wicker chairs. Right outside the tent were two cushy chaise lounges facing the oversized pools, with palm trees and lush tropical landscaping everywhere you looked.

I sat down, looked around, and remembered the hotels we stayed at when I was a kid - the few times we did travel. Typically the pool would be 10' by 20', surrounded by a chain link fence and located next to the parking lot if not *in* the parking lot. There wouldn't be any landscaping; just cement and a fence. I couldn't even imagine then that a place like the Peabody and its pool and grounds existed anywhere except in fairy tales.

At times like this, I often wondered what my father would think if he could see me sitting in this kind of luxury with cost not even a small factor. It was the kind of luxury he'd never experienced even once, and the idea he had to scrimp and struggle his entire life made me sad. I wished he could have known before he passed away how far I had already come.

The cocktail waitress came over and asked me what I wanted.

"What's that one drink that's so popular down here; it's sort of an orange color?" I asked.

"You're thinking of a Planters Punch. We make more of those and Tequila Sunrises than everything else combined."

Tequila, yes!

"I'd like to order two Tequila Sunrises.

"Sure, no problem." The waitress smiled.

"My business associate should be down shortly. Would you wait for her to arrive before you bring the first two drinks?"

"You got it, no problem."

About 20 minutes later, Sandy showed up wearing a white hat, sunglasses, and a yellow beach jacket with a pair of sandals. She looked great, and in this heat the jacket wasn't going to stay on for long.

Sandy was about 5'6", average weight, but well endowed and curvy - the kind of curves you get from your genetics, not from working out. She wasn't super cut muscular wise, but she still looked fit, kind of like a cheerleader's body. She sat down on the chaise lounge next to me without taking off her beach jacket.

Patience my man, patience.

"Here are your drinks, sir."

"Thank you!" I shot our waitress a confident smile.

"Sandy, I think you'll like these. The waitress said that these Tequila Sunrises and a drink called a Planter's Punch are almost all they serve."

"Sure," Sandy said. "When my husband and I were on vacation in the Bahamas two years ago, we just about lived on these, except we would order double tequila."

"That sounds like a good idea. If we have any more I will order them that way. Tell me about your trip to the Bahamas, Sandy," and Yaddi, Yaddi, Yaddi, she was off for about 30 minutes.

I could see the beads of perspiration running down her head and neck. Why didn't she take her beach jacket off? I had already been in the water twice to cool off.

"Another round, sir?" Our attentive waitress had returned.

"Absolutely, thanks, but make them with double tequila if you don't mind."

"Well, time for me to roll over and tan the other side for awhile" I said.

I rolled onto my stomach and put my head down, looking away from Sandy's chair. She couldn't see my smile as I heard the beach jacket come off. I refrained from turning around and looking until the drinks arrived.

"Here are your drinks, sir. Would you like to see a menu or anything?"

"Not for me right now, I'm perfect." I rolled over to ask "How about you, Sandy?"

"No thanks, maybe later."

Sandy had a patterned yellow bathing suit on that was mostly string around her back and up over her shoulders. Her bottom half was more modest, but still was cut high on the sides. The more I saw of her body, the more I liked. I didn't think she was that fit at first, but when I saw her stomach muscles that were now out in the open, I was impressed. This girl was doing some PX90 or Insanity workouts, or something.

There was more Yaddi, Yaddi, Yaddi for another 40 minutes and a third round of drinks. When the fourth round came, so did the time to make my move.

"Wow, Sandy, I think I should have had some lunch after all. I think I better call it an afternoon."

"Yeah, me too." Sandy yawned and stretched lazily.

I motioned to the waitress.

This next part was going to be tricky.

"Sandy, did you bring the compliance file with you?"

Of course I knew she did; that's what we were doing down there.

"Yes, it's in my room."

"Do you mind if I pick it up? I might as well use the time before dinner to read through the details one more time.

For a long time I'd been wondering when I would find a woman I could attach the "Atomic Orgasm" label to. I had finally found her"

2-12 - - The Ambush

"HATCHET MAN: a person hired to perform underhanded or unscrupulous tasks (as ruin reputations)" - Merriam Webster

Our morning meeting with Vince Bennett and Brad Bishop was set for 9:30.

I felt like hell from all the tequila the day before and Sandy *looked* like hell. She had a massive hangover. I had the feeling our previous afternoon might have turned out differently if she had a re-do.

One day she might recall the sweetness of the afternoon, but recalling it from the perspective of a massive headache combined with nausea wasn't going to frame it as one of life's beautiful moments.

After a quick trip to the fruit section of the breakfast buffet, we took a taxi to the suburban office of Affluent Society Insurance in Altamonte Springs, just north of Orlando.

The offices were in a modern 6-story building with updated decor. Not rich or exquisite like you might find at a large law firm or engineering company, but still professional and successful looking.

Our names were on the message board as we walked in to the local Affluent Society Insurance Offices:

WELCOME
BIRCH BENTLEY, SENIOR VICE PRESIDENT
SANDY LOCKHEART, COMPLIANCE MANAGER

"Good morning. My name is Birch Bentley and this is Sandy Lockheart from the Home Office, we have an appointment with Vince Carter."

"I'll let Mr. Carter know you've arrived, Mr. Bentley." The receptionist turned and lifted her receiver.

"Mr. Bentley, welcome to Florida."

Vince was younger than I expected, mid 30's, hair already thinning. He had a nice demeanor about him, and you could tell instantly he was a bright person. I'd seen him at various sales conventions over the years, but never put his name and face together - not surprising since there are almost 1,500 people thrown together for four days and three nights.

We sat down in the conference room, exchanged pleasantries, and got down to business.

"Well, Vince, I guess you know there's a lot of attention in the home office being paid to this situation with Brad."

"I wouldn't doubt that a bit." He shifted uncomfortably in his seat, but kept his face impassive.

"Vince, you know I spent time in the field myself. I was an agent for almost six months as part of our company's 'Fast Start' program. I say that so that you know I have an understanding of what transpires when a policy is sold."

"I'm sure you do, Mr. Bentley and I'm sure you were a good Agent."

"Thanks, Vince. So, tell me exactly why you think the Attorney General of Florida is looking into Brad's sales practices?"

"Mr. Bentley, everyone inside the industry knows about the trouble Brad's former company had here in Florida. There were multiple charges of illegal replacement and huge eventual settlements with hefty fines paid. Brad has become guilty by association."

"Vince, we both know that replacement is legal, but our records show that some of the necessary documentation is missing on several of the replacements Brad handled."

Carter frowned. "Mr. Bentley, in my opinion, the Insurance Commissioner wants to run for Attorney General here in Florida next year, and the way to keep his name out in front of the public is to find more alleged examples of insurance company abuses, and bring in more money from fines and settlements."

"Vince, a replacement without the replacement forms is a technical violation of the law - illegal in virtually every state in the country."

"Yes, that's true, but..."

"There are no buts here, Vince, because the Insurance Commissioner and Attorney General are involved. A technical violation, regardless of how small or infrequent you or Brad thinks, can reflect poorly on all of us because the letter and the spirit of the law are violated."

My tone was firm now, less conversational than previously.

"There isn't any wiggle room on this, Vince. When we bring Brad in here, you're going to tell him that he's being terminated immediately. The actual termination letter will be mailed directly to Brad from Affluent Society Insurance."

"That's going to be hard to do, Mr. Bentley. He has a family and his passion makes him a bit explosive."

"Vince, that's exactly what we're going to do; the decision has been made and is final."

"O.K., Mr. Bentley, I understand I'm not the ultimate decision maker." He looked away as if dissatisfied with the answer but unwilling to press it further.

"Thank you, Vince. May I add one thing? I don't mean to be telling you how to do your job, but I'm sure you care about Brad the same way you care about all the people who work for you - it's what makes you good at your job. Before you call Brad in here, can I relate some advice given to me that I've always appreciated?"

"Sure, go ahead Mr. Bentley."

"Several years ago I had to fire someone who was not only close to me, but who had also been extremely helpful and influential in my career. I sought out some help from an experienced person and this is what he said. First, when that person comes in the room, let him know he's fired before he even finishes sitting in the chair. Second, get him out of that chair as quickly as possible. Commiserating with him serves no useful purpose. Following that advice wasn't easy, Vince, but it was good advice and counsel, and I recommend the same."

I didn't know where my next comments came from. Maybe I thought they would impress Sandy, or maybe I'd been reading too many of my self-help books, or maybe I just had too much coffee that morning.

"Have you ever read Sun Tzu, Vince?"

"Can't say that I have, Mr. Bentley."

"He writes about a principle that I think expresses what I'm trying to say: 'The quality of decision is like the well-timed swoop of a falcon which enables it to strike and destroy its victim.' Be that falcon, Vince, and strike before expected."

Sandy and Vince both looked at me curiously.

I sat there not embarrassed, but frustrated. Nobody appreciated my Sun Tzu quotes; they just didn't *get* them, which was

personally disappointing to me. How can people miss the power behind the words of Sun Tzu?

2-13 - - The Sacrificing Of Brad Bishop

sac·ri·fice (skr-fs) a. The act of offering something to a deity in propitiation or homage, especially the ritual slaughter of an animal or a person.

Brad Bishop was a confident, good looking, likable young man. He'd already achieved at a high level in an industry where maturity is considered essential; losing talent like Brad would be a negative for any company. Brad had a special persona. Anyone could see that he was a star the moment he entered a room.

When he sat down with Vince, Sandy, and I, there wasn't any small talk.

"Brad, this is Birch Bentley and Sandy Lockheart from the Home Office. They have informed me that you are being terminated from your employment with Affluent Society Insurance."

Vince showed he had a spine and had done and said exactly as I had asked him to. *Nicely done*, I thought to myself.

Brad looked at Vince and then looked at me.

"What? Don't I even get a chance to say anything to defend myself?" Brad shot back.

"I'm afraid the decision has been made and is final," Vince told him in a forthright manner.

Vince was impressively showing his toughness.

"What about my clients and my pending commissions?" Brad asked Vince.

"Brad, you understand you're advanced a whole years commissions at the time of sale. When agents quit or are terminated, the procedure is not to pay any additional money until all advances have been paid back."

"That will take several months, and I'm not selling cars – I can't just go out tomorrow and start selling some other company's policies - I have several proposals and un-issued policies pending."

"I'm sorry, Brad, there's really nothing I can do."

"I'm sorry too, Vince, for this kind of bullshit. I'm at least entitled to some kind of explanation."

"Perhaps Mr. Bentley from the Home Office can provide a better explanation than I can."

I was unprepared for Vince to hand me the ball.

"Brad, first let me explain that I'm sorry..."

"Sorry my ass, you come down here and put Vince up to this. I've known Vince for two years. Do you think I don't know what's going on here? You're nothing but a hatchet man; no offense meant to you ma'am."

I glanced over at Sandy, and she looked even sicker than she had earlier that morning.

I looked Brad squarely in the eyes.

"Brad, let's keep this respectful. Look, I'm sorry that you didn't follow the exact procedures for replacing policies, but rules are rules, you have to live by them and we have to live by them; our hands are tied."

Brad's next words started loud and ended with him shouting.

"I don't want to hear all your crap about rules. I went through this in great detail with the people from the insurance commissioner's office - there was no material misrepresentation. Everyone who purchased a new policy had full knowledge of what they were buying. This is undeserved, and I'm not going to accept it,"

Brad was now past the point of passionate. He was into that explosive stage Vince had warned us about. He was leaning in and making direct eye contact with me. His stare was threatening; his body language was flashing aggression. It was time to end this.

"Brad, I'm sorry but the decision has been made and is final."

As I said this I rose from my chair to signal that the meeting was over. I knew how to end a meeting: you stand up, preferably while you are talking.

As much as Brad might have wanted to sit there and debate what was fair and just, I certainly had no intention of re-hashing his termination any more.

Inside I felt sorry for him and my gut was tightening because he was getting the shaft. He obviously didn't fully understand the potential consequences of not doing a complete paperwork job; a common fault of great salespeople.

The worst thing at that particular moment would have been to show Brad some sympathy.

My head said I had a job to do - solve the problem right then and there, which I had just done, and there wasn't going to be a debate – the meeting was over regardless of how Brad, Vince, or I felt about it.

Brad stood up facing me, his 6'3" frame matching mine. For a second I thought there might be a physical confrontation, which would have been a very poor choice for him.

He turned to leave and on his way out he grabbed the chair next to him and launched it about six feet into the glass wall of the conference room, shattering the glass. Anybody on the other side could have been seriously cut.

"This is complete and utter bullshit and I will fight it; you can count on it" Brad promised on the way out.

A high-profile legal fight at this point of the merger talks with ALH was the last thing I needed to be responsible for.

After Brad disappeared down the hall I grabbed my briefcase and escorted Sandy out around the broken glass at our feet.

I needed to talk with Vince before I left, but didn't think Sandy was going to be up to participating in the conversation. She looked pale. I was worried she might throw up at any second, making matters worse.

"Sandy, I need to talk with Vince for a minute. Would you mind waiting for me in the building foyer downstairs?"

"I'd be glad to," and she hurriedly exited the office to escape the tension.

Inside Vince's office I had to break the bad news to him.

"Vince, you've done a good job for Affluent Society Insurance, but this problem with the Insurance Commissioner's office fell under your watch and you own it. HR has prepared an exit package for you that I think you'll find is fair but I need your resignation by the end of this week."

I handed Vince a file with his exit package papers.

"I'm sorry, Vince, this is not personal, it's just business."

It would have been fun to say this in my Godfather voice. I do a pretty good one, but sadly this was not the time or place.

Vince didn't say anything because there was nothing for him to say. He was smart enough to know he was out, and that there would be no sense saying or doing anything that might negatively impact whatever was being offered in the envelope I had just handed to him. He grasped that his career with Affluent Society was through, taking the news a lot better than Brad Bishop had.

Once outside, I fell into one of my really bad habits: trying to use humor to ease the pressure. Unfortunately, I'm no Jerry Seinfeld, and many times I make the situation worse.

"Sandy, when we get back let's be sure to tell admin not to use any more glass walls in conference rooms."

Sandy didn't say anything.

I looked at her face. Her lips were tightly pursed and you didn't have to have a degree in psychoanalytics to see she was obviously distraught, which caused me some concern.

One of my strengths is reading people, knowing what they're thinking and feeling. I knew exactly how Sandy was feeling, but I didn't know if this new distance between us had to do with what happened yesterday, today, or both.

I'm a student of association. I'm diligent about not having people associate unpleasant emotions with me if I can avoid it. It's more than not being negative; it's a deeper understanding of the physiology of the brain. Don't put people in mental states that are downbeat in your presence. There's no gain to it.

In retrospect I should have left Sandy at the hotel while I had all the firing fun and picked her up before our meeting with the compliance people.

"What time is our appointment with the people from the Insurance Department, Sandy?"

"12:30." Her tone was flat, without any warmth or feeling to it.

I looked down at my Movado; the time was 10:05. The meeting had only lasted about 40 minutes. I decided to try to repair my connection with Sandy.

"I'll probably be talking too much at lunch to really eat much. Let's go over to that Starbucks we passed - I'm going to get one of their oatmeal's. Food always tastes better after a good firing, don't you think?"

Another poor, and failed, attempt at humor.

This was all for show, because I absolutely hated firing most people. Except in those few cases where people really deserved to be cut loose, terminations were the worst part of any job.

Some people wear their emotions on their sleeves but I could not afford to be one of them. I wore a mask that on the outside read Senior Vice President of Affluent Society Insurance. I was expected to act a certain way and do the company's bidding. I cloaked what I thought and carried out the company pretext; for now at least.

2-14 - - Vince Carter

When Birch Bentley sat down in my office, I knew immediately - here was another jackass from the home office.

Blockheads like him could never make it in the field selling insurance, but they fly into town like they know everything and look down their noses at the people putting the revenue numbers on the scoreboard.

He spent six months in the field. What a laugh. Those kinds of assignments are nothing but going and sitting in a sales office for six months and getting in everybody's way.

Just once I'd like to tell one of these morons from corporate headquarters what I think, but these guys are too stupid to even know when they're being insulted.

How does it make sense to fire one of their top agents and top managers for some minor confusion over paperwork?

They are idiots propped up by people who actually work at their jobs. Birch Bentley and his kind do more destruction than they do good.

I'll take my severance package and find another company to hire me. I'll recruit Brad Bishop and probably half of the rest of the agents here in our office, leaving the Orlando Affluent Society office a shell of what it is now.

Everything will be fine until the home office jackasses from that company start sticking their nose into things.

2-15 - - Sandy Lockheart

When Birch Bentley told me I would be going to Florida with him, I could hardly believe my luck. He was so handsome and powerful, with beautiful hands. I wasn't sure if he was interested in me or just interested in my relationships with the people in the Florida Insurance Department.

When he called me down to his office for a meeting I gave him a good look at my legs. I was pretty sure he was interested because he couldn't look away. When he went to take a telephone call I gave him another view to think about.

Once we got to Florida he wanted to go down to the pool right away. I wasn't there two minutes before he had a drink in my hand. That was a good sign. I was ready before the tequila but the sun and drinks had me spinning. When we got to my room all I could do was wait for it to happen.

I feigned a little bit of resistance but not much. He gave me more sexual enjoyment in one afternoon than I had all the previous year combined.

Once I was satisfied and sobered up I felt differently about it; a little ashamed and humiliated that I had let him use me. I needed the sex but not in so cheap a manner; in a hotel room in Florida with a man I hardly knew. I felt dirty, taken advantage of, even though I'd been a more than willing participant.

I was also horrified by the way he fired those two poor men in Florida, making some nasty comment about a falcon swooping down or something. Did he have even an ounce of empathy?

I was going to sort it all out when I got back to New York and felt better. Right then all I wanted to do was go purge all the poison that was in my body.

2-16 - - The Politics Of Regulation

"What I'd like to say is 'that regulation,' why don't you stick 'that regulation' where the sun doesn't shine?" - - Birch Bentley

At lunch we were meeting with two representatives from the Florida Insurance Department; June Rivera from compliance who was Sandy's contact, and Allison Rohn from legal.

Allison had taken the liberty to also invite Renee Hatfield from the Attorney General's office. This was surprising and not a good signal.

After some small talk and placing the order, I informed them that Affluent Society Insurance was in the process of terminating Brad Bishop, and his supervisor, Vince Bennett. I conveyed my belief that would end the investigation into twisting allegations by Affluent Society Insurance. I caught Allison Rohn glancing at Renee Hatfield as I was explaining this.

"Birch, the Insurance Commissioner will be glad to hear you share his conviction that any illegal practices need to be dealt with swiftly and harshly. To comment on any pending investigations however, would be premature and also inappropriate."

"Renee, can you tell me this? Is there an official position as it relates to the Insurance Commissioner's office and Affluent Society Insurance?"

"Birch, officially the Insurance Commissioner has done a preliminary investigation and has turned the matter over to the Attorney Generals' office. Any decision now will be made by the Attorney General."

"Well, I think I can say that Affluent Society Insurance will be more than happy to provide whatever else the Attorney General may need.

Sure, Al would only be too happy to fly any incriminating evidence down personally.

Government people in general and Regulators specifically scare the hell out of me because if they decide to become

unreasonable, there is no recourse. In addition they are not motivated by the same things the rest of society is motivated by; reward. You just have to hope you will deal with one of the good ones and pray you don't ever get one of the bad ones on your back.

We still had a few minutes before our food arrived. I decided to speak with Jill in legal and see if there was a question or two I could ask at lunch that would be helpful.

"Would you excuse me for a moment, there is one call I was supposed to return at exactly one o'clock?

I called Jill Mahoney from legal.

"Jill, this is Birch Bentley."

"Birch, I thought you were having lunch with the people from the Department of Insurance?"

"I am. The reason I am calling you is Allison Rohn from the legal department of the Insurance Commissioner's office has invited a Renee Hatfield from the Attorney General's office to lunch with us."

"That's strange."

"That's what I thought - what do you think her presence means?"

"One thing a person from the AG office at your lunch means for sure is that we're not exactly invisible, and confirms you did the right thing by terminating Brad Bishop. Also the investigation, as it relates to Affluent Society Insurance, is probably broader than Brad Bishop."

"Jill, you just said what I didn't want to even think. I'm trying to think if there is anything I can do here at lunch?"

Look, whatever happens isn't going to play out there at lunch. Be statesmen like, and try not to offer any specific information you don't have to. I'm working on the flip side of this through some

contacts we have via our PAC and that isn't going to involve the people you are with today."

"Right, Jill, I'll be in touch. Thanks."

When I got back to the table our food had just been served.

"Great timing, Birch" Sandy said as they put her salad in front of her.

I wasn't really that hungry, and this was a great opportunity to lead the conversation.

"You probably take this weather for granted down here, but let me tell you what it's like back in New York in February...."

It's so cold the Brooklyn Bridge is freezing its nuts off. No can't use that one.

It's so cold that I saw a lawyer with his hands in his own pockets for once. No, I think Renee has a law degree.

"The street performers have thrown away their castanets - they're just using their chattering teeth!"

That got a small polite laugh but apparently there wasn't going to be much to talk about other than the weather.

When the check came, our guests insisted on separate checks - as a regulator and government employee, they had strict guidelines for avoiding even the suggestion of any undue influence. I paid for Sandy's and my lunch, and we went back to the hotel to pick up our things for our late afternoon flight back to New York.

3) The Hamptons

3-1 - - The Invitation

"Never open the door to a lesser evil, for other and greater ones invariably slink in after it." - - *Baltasar Gracián (1601 - 1658), The Art of Worldly Wisdom*

An Important day was about to be celebrated at Affluent Society; Donald Hightower's 60th birthday. Everybody knew this because there was a company campaign in his honor called '60 Improvements in 60 Days.'

I wasn't sure why we needed to honor his birthday; we didn't honor anybody else's. Suggestions were collected and there was a committee to select the best idea with, of course, Al Perri in charge of the committee.

There was a prize of $1,000.00 for the best suggestion but you could also make your suggestion anonymously.

I wanted to be seen as participating so I suggested we improve the appearance of the entrance to our building with a red canopy that had our logo on it, and some cement planters with shrubbery. It was chosen as one of the 60.

I also suggested the company improve the coffee but didn't put my name to the suggestion. Our coffee was shit. I don't know why it is that the coffee tastes so bad in so many places. It's not that hard to get coffee right. I bring a Starbucks to work with me every day.

There was going to be cake sent to each floor and served in the dining hall, blah, blah, blah. The truth is nobody gave a rat's ass about Donald Hightower's birthday, but we all had to play along like it was some big deal; a joyous celebration and one of our happiest days of the year. If he really wanted us to appreciate his birthday he should have given everybody the day off so they could spend time with their families, or do something they *wanted* to do.

Nobody gave twaddle because Donald Hightower was one of the least personable people in the world. He was rarely visible and when he was, he looked like he was mad. If you happened to pass him in the hall or see him in the common elevators, he didn't acknowledge your presence. If you said hello he responded with a half nod and looked away - as if he was upset that he had to make an effort to greet you and blow you off at the same time.

He didn't bother with even a thin veil of personality to anyone; at least not around the office.

That's why I was so surprised to receive an invitation to the birthday bash he was having at his personal residence in the Hamptons.

"Al, did you receive an invitation to Mr. Hightower's party at his home?"

"Yes, how did you hear about it?"

How did I hear about it? Was it a secret? I wasn't sure I liked the tone of his question and decided not to tell him yet that I was on the guest list.

"I heard somebody up on his floor mention it."

"It's going to be a big deal; lots of important high society people and incredibly exclusive."

"Are you taking Marla, Al?"

"Don't have any choice."

What an asshole.

"Sounds like a fun evening, Al."

I went back to my office, opened Google Maps and typed in the address on Dune Road listed on the invitation. Hightower didn't have a *house*; he had a palatial estate, right on the beach. The property was in Southampton with water on both sides: the Atlantic Ocean on one side and Mecox Bay on the other.

I went to the Zillow website and couldn't find a valuation for Hightower's house, but found a comparable one at $17 million. I suspected Hightower's location made his home worth even more.

I wondered how, even with a salary of three and a half million a year, Hightower could afford a house in the twenty mil range.

I looked at the invitation again and dress was formal. I decided I was going to deck myself out with a completely new tux and accessories. In a way, this was going to be a coming out party for me. Even though I had been to gala events in the city surrounded by the high society types, this was going to be my first society event at a private estate in the Hamptons. I was going to make the best of it.

The party was only a week away which made me a last minute add-on; but I didn't care and I didn't mention to Perri that I would be going.

3-2 - - The Move

"To every thing there is a season, and a time to every purpose under the heaven" - - Ecclesiastes 3

I received the invitation on Friday - one week and a day prior to the Saturday event.

The next day I had dinner plans with Jennifer, which would be the perfect time to pop the question.

Not the marriage question; the 'is it time to sleep together?' question.

"Guess what I received in the mail this week, Jennifer."

"I don't know; an invitation to a White House dinner?"

"That's incredibly close for not having any clues. It's an invitation to our CEO's sixtieth birthday party at his beachside estate in Southampton. It's going to be incredibly exclusive."

"I've been to a few of those in connection with my work. They're a great place to people watch. Someone wrote that the rich are different. I don't know if that's true, but their Hampton parties are different; that's for sure."

"It was F. Scott Fitzgerald. I'm thinking about going up Friday and staying through to Sunday. I've never been to the Hamptons."

"You're kidding! You'll love it but to be honest, it's a lot more fun in the summer than it is now."

"I was wondering if we're far enough along in our relationship that I could take you along? We could stay in a cozy bed and breakfast and have a nice dinner Friday evening. On Saturday we could take in the shops and have lunch on the water somewhere."

"Are we talking one room or two?" She looked coy.

"You tell me, Jennifer."

"That's not the kind of question a nice girl should have to answer this soon into a relationship."

There was the 'this soon' thing again. If you don't want to go with me maybe I'll ask Brenda.

"No problem, Jennifer, I'll make the decision, one room."

"Now you're being a little presumptive aren't you?"

"Jennifer, we're adults, let's do one room."

"Let me think about; I'll let you know."

3-3 - - The Missus

"Keep a strict watch over an unruly wife, lest, finding an opportunity, she use it. - -The Book of the All-Virtuous Wisdom of Joshua ben Sira

I rented a car, and Jennifer and I drove out to our hotel in Southampton on Friday afternoon. She'd used her travel connections to book us a local bed and breakfast place named the 1708 House.

We were booked into Room 3 and it had a king-sized bed, a seating alcove and a desk. The bathroom had one of those claw-footed bathtubs with a separate shower. It also had something I'd never seen before, a heated towel rack, which made the towels feel like they just came out of the dryer.

Friday night we had a nice dinner and went back to the room. We were, surprisingly, a little awkward together; but the ice had been broken.

On Saturday morning we tried again and the awkwardness had left the room.

We had lunch, shopped, and left for the event at 6:30 to arrive at 6:45. We didn't want to be the first ones to arrive, standing around with our hands in our pockets waiting for everyone to get there.

We pulled up to the front of the house and there was a line of about ten cars waiting for valet service. It was a little unwieldy because the valets didn't have that much room to turn the cars around in.

With several valets, however, it didn't take too long for our turn and a person with a clipboard came to the driver's window.

"Name, please?"

"Bentley is the last name; Birch Bentley."

The attendant seemed to be having trouble finding my name until he flipped to what looked like the last page.

"Here it is. Please leave your keys in the car and take this ticket." He wrote my name on the ticket. "There will be a person on the porch when you're ready to leave who will retrieve your car for you."

Jennifer and I went up the walkway to the house. There were little white lights in all the trees and bushes that outlined their forms. The landscaping looked incredible, even for February.

There was a greeter at the door and I had to give my name again.

The inside exceeded my expectations in several ways but didn't exceed them in others. It wasn't as big as I thought it might be, although there was a huge foyer. To our right was a half living room, half ball room obviously designed with entertaining in mind. The far wall of the ball room was glass from floor to ceiling and although I couldn't see anything right then, I knew it faced out to the ocean and was probably really impressive in the daylight.

The foyer had one of the shiniest, most polished tiles I'd ever seen. It was an elegant earth tone beige marble with interspersed rippled bands that were darker in color. The tiles were the big pieces, not the one foot squares, and there were small diagonal black offsetting squares about every three to four feet. It made you look down rather than up at the oversized chandelier.

Standing in the beautiful foyer with a view into the ball room was close to awe-inspiring.

It was lavishly decorated with art objects of obvious high quality on the table tops and paintings on the walls. Hightower's choice in paintings was consistent. He liked bright paintings of all types with few sharp lines so your imagination could fill in the details. His taste in art surprised me and was close to my own. I recognized one as a Leroy Neiman and I couldn't imagine in a house like this it was anything but an original.

There were service people everywhere. This was *not* the house or party of someone who was struggling financially in any way, and I wondered again how he was doing it on three and a half million a year. Especially because I had heard from Perri he had a nice place in the city as well that was worth six million.

$25 million is a lot of real estate to pay for on an underpaid insurance company CEO's salary.

"Birch, I didn't expect to see you here."

It was Al Perri making me feel welcome in his special way.

"Hi, Al, I received an invitation last week, didn't I tell you?"

"No, and Hightower didn't mention it to me either."

"I don't know, Al; my name was on the list."

I didn't tell him it was on the last page, and I was now sure I'd been included at the last minute, but Al was pissing me off. It wasn't his party and he was making Jennifer and I feel uncomfortable, like we didn't belong there.

"Al, I think you've met Jennifer."

Jennifer reached out to shake Al's hand.

"I could never forget a face like this," Al said as he looked at Jennifer. "If Birch is smart he'll hold your hand tonight and not let go."

Whatever, Al, you schmuck. What's the implication; someone with tons of money is more appealing to Jennifer then I am?

"Where's Marla, Al?"

Al obviously wasn't following the advice he'd just dished out to me. I guess he wasn't worried about someone stealing Marla.

"She's around; I think some of the ladies went on a tour of the house."

"Well I'll look for her and be sure to tell her hello. Jennifer, would you like to walk over to the bar with me and see what they have to drink?"

Al still had a bit of a puzzled look on his face like he wanted to question me some more but let it go.

"Birch, you looked a little tense talking to Al." Jennifer sounded concerned.

"You could tell?"

"Definitely."

"He's my boss and I always have conflict issues with bosses. It's a family curse."

"What will you have, sir?" The bartender waited expectantly as an attractive brunette wearing a deep burgundy dress and fabulous jewels walked by distracting my attention.

"Two Chardonnays please."

"Jennifer, this is what I want. The expensive house, the ornaments that go with it, the lifestyle; it's what I've been striving a long time for. This is the zip code I want to live in."

"You'll get it, Birch, it doesn't happen overnight."

"I know that, but I don't know how to express this other than to say I will *not* let anything get in my way of having wealth; for me it's as important as having air to breathe."

"I have faith in you, Birch; your drive is obvious to people."

We met a few people and my conversation was more guarded than normal. I didn't ask a lot questions and stuck to talking about the house, the Jets and the Nets, unless something else was brought up.

Jennifer recognized a business client and went off to say hello.

People were wandering all over the house and I heard someone say there was a great view from the rounded veranda off the office. I decided to take a look. I went up the extra wide staircase and walked through the open door of Hightower's home office.

He had a big, expensive desk. One wall was a library, another wall had an oversized fireplace and the far wall had windows and a door facing the ocean. I was conflicted between going outside to admire the view or looking to see what books Hightower had on his bookshelf.

"It's cold out there," I heard somebody say from behind me.

I turned around. It was Donald Hightower's wife, Jacqueline; his second wife actually. I met her twice when she was in the city at our Affluent Society offices.

"I heard the view from the veranda was remarkable and thought I would brave the cold."

"Go ahead if you like. I'm glad you received our invitation and were able to make it."

"Thank you, it was thoughtful of you and Mr. Hightower to extend the invitation. By the way, your house is beautiful, and what a tremendous location."

"It is, isn't it? It's been in the Hightower family for three generations now."

That explained one thing I'd been wondering about; actually, it explained a lot of things including his aloofness, arrogance, and

disdain for people he thinks are below him. I didn't resent his rich upbringing, in fact I envied it; but I didn't understand why it made some people feel they were better than other people. My uncle who's in real estate used to say *"Some people are born on third base and think they've hit a triple."*

"Here you are, Jacqueline."

I looked up and Hightower was coming through the doorway to the office with a look that was hard to read. I couldn't tell if he was surprised to see me there, surprised to see Jacqueline and me together in his office, or both.

"Mr. Bentley was just about to admire the view from your lookout point, dear."

"Go ahead, Birch, if you'd like, but you can't see much at night and it's cold out there; especially with the wind."

It didn't sound like he really wanted me to go out there and I begged off.

"No worries, I have a beautiful girl I brought with me downstairs somewhere; I think I should go find her."

"Good idea, Birch, you don't want to leave a beautiful girl unattended in this crowd. Enjoy the party."

I walked down the stairs, disappointed I hadn't seen the veranda or the books. I looked back up at Jacqueline Hightower who had stepped out of the office and was watching me from the hallway railing outside the office. It had to be her who added me to the invitation list. *Why* she added me was a scary and dangerous thought.

3-4 - - The Billionaire

"A wise man should have money in his head, but not in his heart." - - Jonathan Swift

I found Jennifer downstairs. She was still talking to someone who I found out later was one of her big clients. He was one of the

100

most beautiful men I have ever seen. Dressed in his tuxedo, he looked like he should be on the cover of GQ, and he and Jennifer seemed to be getting along well.

They were laughing hard with Jennifer's hand on his arm like she was trying to make him stop because she didn't want her makeup to run.

I walked on over.

"Somebody must have said something funny."

Jennifer spoke up.

"Oh, Birch, this is Sunny. He's one of our clients at our agency."

"Jennifer has told me a lot about you, Birch. I'm glad to finally meet you."

"Then you have me at a disadvantage, Sunny, because I don't know anything about you, but I'm pleased to meet you. It seems we both have first names out of the ordinary. Is Sunny your real name?"

"Just a nickname people call me around the office."

"Is there a story behind it?"

"There is; one of my co-workers had a horse named Sunny and I told him I liked the name. The word got around about what I said and before long everyone was calling me Sunny. What about you, Birch; are you named after a tree?"

"Sunny, did I see a smirk go across your face when you just asked me that?"

"I can't deny it; you probably did, but no offense was meant. I was smiling because I thought I was being clever."

"You know what, Sunny, I like clever, truthfully, and as a matter of fact I was named after a specific kind of tree by my

mother. What I wasn't named after was a horse. Were you named after the whole horse or perhaps just a specific part of a horse? You know; the part the tail's connected to?"

Sunny & Jennifer laughed and then I joined them laughing myself.

"Very good, Birch."

What do you do, Sunny?"

"Hedge funds, investment stuff; and you're in insurance Jennifer said?"

"Affluent Society."

"I have some of my personal insurance with your company, Birch."

"Now that we have all that out of the way, let's all go get another drink" Jennifer said.

3-5 - - A Lowly Caretaker

Question: In word games, what is a four letter word for a lowly worker? Answer: Peon

When Sunny found someone else to charm, Jennifer told me more about him.

"Birch, Sunny made a name for himself starting a successful hedge fund right out of Harvard. Everyone says he's already a billionaire."

Jennifer spotted the owner of her company, Abdul Khiref.

"Abdul, I didn't know you would be here. Birch, this is Abdul Khiref, Abdul, this is Birch Bentley."

We shook hands and sized each other up.

Abdul was telling a small group about his new place in Central Park West. From what he was describing, his place had to be approaching seven or eight million in value. I had my doubts that he earned that much money from his agency that Jennifer had told me so much about; a successful but not a large business.

I remembered that Jennifer told me his family was from Iran. The timing of his move to America meant the chances were his family had probably been part of, or connected to, the Shah. I had read about a member of what was the royal family, before the Ayatollah took over things, who had 39 brothers and sisters - all of them educated in Europe and the U.S. This was another guy born on third base, starting life with a family fortune.

Also in the group we were talking to was a distinguished gentleman who had something to do with the U.N., I didn't really catch his title. There was also a tobacco importer from Egypt. Now *there's* a useful contributor to our society. U.S. cigarette companies bought the cheaper Egyptian tobacco to mix it in with the more expensive, U.S. grown tobacco.

I looked over at Jennifer while the conversation continued. She was intelligent, she was beautiful, she had grace and style, she was engaging and entertaining - but she had not yet achieved on the level of the other people in the room. Still, she was not intimidated by anyone there. She fit the environment we were in like she had been surrounded by opulence her entire life.

The conversation turned to politics and then the Eurodollar and eventually rolled around to leadership, with Abdul blessing us with his formula for success.

"My approach is to set objectives and give people authority to go after those objectives. I hold them accountable for their performance so I don't have to get into the detailed management. If they don't perform then I get somebody else."

Here was my chance to participate and show how smart I was.

"Where is the leader's accountability? What if the objectives set by the leader were the problem or even the selection of the person put in charge, not the implementation of those objectives?"

"What do you mean, exactly?" asked Abdul with only the slightest hint of annoyance on his face.

"If someone a leader selected and gave a set of objectives to failed; wasn't the failure of the leader's subordinates also to some degree the failure of the leader?"

I was relatively sure he wouldn't take this personally, just as a rhetorical question. I continued to demonstrate my worldly knowledge.

"In Japan, I'm told, the person in charge takes responsibility for the success or failure of everyone in his group."

Abdul's response made me realize the gap between his thinking and my thinking.

"In business, success or failure is measured in profits; final accountability is either the gain or loss of money. Do you understand money and its relationship to power, my young friend?"

This was also a rhetorical question that he wasn't waiting for me to answer.

"Here in the U.S., it is said that you can rise to fortune and position, HAH! In much of the world, your fortune is your position - and it's true here too - how many of your Rockefellers, Fords, Kennedys have no position, no station? How many of your country's poor people go to Harvard, Yale, or Stanford?"

I was in the thick of it now.

"Yes, you're right, but many people from humble backgrounds have amassed huge fortunes, or even become President."

He lectured me again.

"You are missing the point;" *imbecile* was implied but left off the end of the sentence. "Fewer people with fortunes become poor than poor people become rich. If you don't have a fortune, get a

fortune; then you can make the rules. As I was saying before, my rule is you either meet my objectives or I will replace you."

"What if you don't have a fortune?"

"Then that is your problem; and people who already have a fortune are not going to worry about your problem."

This was blunt but there it was; the truth. I hadn't just learned something as much as I was reminded of it. Nobody besides me really cared about my fortune, or should I say lack of it, especially the people that already had one.

Abdul's comments cut through me like a knife. I was surrounded by wealth and none of it was mine. If I wanted a share I would have to fight for it because the people that had it weren't going to give it up easily.

I began to feel a little out of place. I was a manager surrounded by owners; a caretaker of sorts. A replaceable part to be discarded at will. I had come a long way but I was nowhere near the league most of these people were in.

I had stepped on my own dick, but Jennifer came to my rescue.

"Birch, I need to refresh my drink; care to join me? Gentlemen, would you excuse us?"

"Thanks, Jennifer."

"Birch, pay these people no mind. They have money; that is all."

"I know that, Jennifer, it's just that tonight has been a gentle slap in the face reminder that I have a lot of mountain left to climb."

3-6 - - Social Graces

"Lack of mastery of the social graces reveals what you are." - - Birch Bentley

Jennifer and I refreshed our drinks and the last person at the party I wanted to talk to came over.

"Jennifer, this is Jacqueline Hightower, our hostess."

"Jennifer, I am soooo pleased to meet you. Do you mind if I borrow this handsome young man of yours for a moment? There is somebody I promised I would introduce him to."

"Not at all, Mrs. Hightower."

Jacqueline tucked her arm in mine and led me away from Jennifer.

Shit, this was going to get me fired. Either I rejected our hostess or our host would see me with his wife's arm in mine, with her breast pressed up against my bicep, and really be pissed. I should have had Jennifer go with us but it happened too fast for me to react.

In reality it was Jacqueline Hightower that had exhibited the inadequate social graces; but I was stuck with the consequences.

"I don't see who I'm looking for, Birch, but while I have you, let me ask you a question."

She was still hanging on to my arm and I could feel that she had a great curve to her body that was hidden by the dress she was wearing. She was probably about 40; twenty years or so younger than her husband. I didn't know how many years they'd been married, just that she was his second wife and fit all the stereotypes of the expression - trophy wife.

"There's going to be a charitable event one of the women's groups I am involved in is organizing. It's a dinner we're having for our Junior High School Achievement Group. I wonder if you would be willing to come up and give a short talk on what you do at Affluent Society?"

I should address the group and not her husband? What are Hightower and Perri going to say if they get wind of this? *Beg off.*

"Well, I would have to check the dates and find out more about the talk you need, but if everything worked out, of course, I'd be happy to."

I didn't know the dates but I already knew I'd be booked out of town; out of the country would be even better.

I looked up and saw Donald Hightower making his way over to us. He didn't look like he was enjoying his birthday party at all at that particular moment.

3-7 - - The Gift

"When somebody gives you something, be gracious." - - Birch Bentley

"Jacqueline, they're about to light the candles on the cake." His tone seemed irked with a steely undertone.

"Of course, Donald, I was just asking Birch..."

Don't say it, Jacqueline, don't say it.

"Jacqueline, we should get over there right now. Birch, please excuse us."

I found Jennifer exactly where I had left her.

"What was that all about?" she said in a way that I knew she was being a good sport about being left alone.

"I'll tell you later, Jennifer." I didn't want to make a big deal about it right then.

A big table with a huge cake had been brought into the foyer and everyone crowded around it in a circle. The lights were turned down and we all sang Happy Birthday to Don, Donald, Mr. Hightower.

He made a wish and blew out seven candles, one for every ten years and one for luck, and everyone applauded.

Then Al Perri went and stood by Hightower and began to sing "For he's a jolly good fellow."

What a suck up.

The invitation said not to bring presents, but there was a box on the table that was from Jacqueline. She was beaming with the kind of anticipation as if she was the one who would be receiving the present.

Hightower carefully opened the box and pulled out... I don't know what.

It was some kind of sculpture that sort of looked like a modern art version of a Remington Western statue, but a better description would be a mouse with a cowboy hat riding a rat.

Hightower put it down and said "Thank you, honey," giving her a small peck on the cheek.

Okay, maybe it did look like a cowboy mouse on a rodent, but how much trouble would it have been to act pleased by it?

He could have been thankful for the thought if not the gift. He could have held it up and made a big deal about it, asked who the artist was, seen if there was a story behind it, given her a big hug and tell her he would find a special place for it. In some circles the sculpture or whatever it was must have been valued as chic.

He didn't do anything but cheapen her efforts.

3-7 - - The Reward

"Sex is its own reward." - - Birch Bentley

I turned to Jennifer and resisted the urge to say anything about what just happened.

"Are you about ready to leave; this party has been disappointing to say the least?"

"How about we head back to our room, Birch, and I'll make you forget all about the Hightower's and their kind."

"Let's go."

On the way out the door I ran into board member, Phil Justus.

"Birch, were you able to get me those tickets for the, Nets, Spurs, game in March?"

"Phil, I know I've told the right people to make sure our box is reserved for your group. On Monday I will call you and confirm but I know you're all set.

"Thanks, Birch, I really appreciate it."

We had luxury boxes at Citi Field, MetLife Stadium, and Madison Square Garden. Al didn't like sports and I never knew where Hightower went; somewhere where I wasn't invited. That left me as the highest ranking person in the company to dole out the tickets.

I didn't waste them on customers or employees until I knew no one on the Board wanted them. I made notes of who liked what teams and checked the schedules months in advance. If someone grew up in San Francisco and the 49ers were going to be in town, they were going to be in the box.

Early planning, my rank, and commitment to buttress my relationship with the Board worked to ensure nobody was going to trump my choices.

If the circus or icecapades were going to be in town, I loaded up the box with the Board's grandchildren and overfed them with popcorn, hot dogs, and an eye-popping dessert cart that people wouldn't believe unless they actually saw it.

As a kid I was ecstatic to be sitting in the left field upper deck with some peanuts and a Coke once a year. I couldn't even conceive of a luxury box with a desert cart that was embarrassingly over the top with fancy delicacies; the perfect vision of excess.

I would talk to Board members about their favorite causes and made sure our charitable giving included gifts in their name and Affluent Society's name. Was someone on an alumni committee heading up a special fund-raising project? No problem, I told them. I would personally see what could be done.

People who make their way to the top often stop doing what got them there. I was determined if I became Chairman and CEO that I would pay even closer attention to the Board then I did right then. I would never let some junior get all the glory for the perks that were handed out.

I was lucky enough to have arrived at a place to distribute the booty, and fortunate Al and Hightower were coasting. 'When the cat's asleep, the mice dance,' - and the Board Members were my favorite dance partners.

Hightower's and Perri's abandonment combined with my nurturing of Board relationships had developed into an influential weapon for me, one that was becoming more dominant every month. I was becoming a visible leader of the company in the eyes of the Board, the people that mattered the most when it came to company succession.

3-8 - - Jennifer Sable

When I met Birch I was overwhelmed. He seemed to have it all together. He was successful at work, good looking, sensitive, with a great sense of humor.

His sayings his mother had taught him resonated deeply with me. I thought anybody who was raised hearing those kinds of messages had to have a good heart.

I knew a man like him had needs, and there were probably a lot of girls who would jump at the chance to satisfy those needs. I didn't want to be one of those kinds of girls. In my entire life I had been with only one other man, and he turned out to be a no good cheating two-timer.

It was conflicting for me. I didn't want to lose Birch, but I didn't want to go against my character and morals either. The more we were together the more I came to see what I thought was his goodness and integrity.

I started to really care for him and a switch flipped - I knew I had to do something because he was the kind of man who was going to get what he wanted somewhere. Brenda would have slept with him in a New York minute. It'd be so great if all girls would get together and hold out until they marry us. Everyone would be getting married in their early twenties again.

While I was debating about which way to go, he asked me to stay the weekend in the Hamptons with him. I wasn't sorry afterward, but I didn't feel good about it either.

When he asked me to go to the Hamptons with him I knew I had to make a choice. I decided he was worth the risk. I liked him a lot and I knew the potential to like him a lot more was there. I allowed myself to think that it was possible we would marry one day, although I would never mention that to Birch.

I hate to say I sacrificed myself but I consider that I did. My decision, if I thought I had a choice, would have been to wait until marriage before having intercourse; but that just isn't how it works today. If you don't sleep with a man he isn't going to stick around. The risk is that he may not stick around anyhow, but holding out was an absolute losing move. So I slept with him.

Once I did it broke a lot of the ice and opened up an entirely new phase of our relationship. I felt he'd rather be with me than be anywhere else and I think that was something he had never experienced before.

When we went to his bosses' party I could see how upset he was that he didn't think he was making the financial progress he thought he should. It made me want to mother him and tell him everything was going to be fine.

I even asked my friend, Sunny Taylor, if there was anything he could do to help Birch understand that all good things would come in time, and that he should relax and enjoy the journey.

3-9 - - Jacqueline Hightower

I know I shouldn't have invited Birch Bentley to Don's birthday party, but I'm so bored with the regular crowd. When Don asks me I'll tell him I thought he told me to include Birch on the invitation list.

I imagine that a tall drink of water like Birch Bentley knows the joy of exuberance. He still gets it, and has it, and I want that kind of person closer in my life.

I'm not talking about sleeping with him; not that the idea of being in bed with him repulses me in any way. I just want people like him in my proximity on a regular basis.

4) Slaying The Dragons

4-1 - - The One Thing

"Clever people always seem to know the one thing that will hook you in." - - Birch Bentley

Monday morning I called up Lana Lang to end things between us.

"Birch, I've left several messages for you. Is everything okay?"

Lana made a good show of playing the concerned sweetheart.

"Lana, there's a reason I haven't called you back. The truth is I've started seeing someone."

"I understand, Birch, I figured it might be something like that when I didn't hear from you."

"Thank you for understanding, Lana, relationships are difficult to predict."

"Relationships are difficult in a lot of ways, Birch. I'm disappointed because I like you a lot."

"Things might have worked out differently under other circumstances, Lana."

"Birch, I gave this some thought while I was wondering if there was someone else. You could still see me if you want. I mean you don't have to give me up completely just because you have another person you like. I'm not the jealous type at all."

That was the one thing Lana could say that had the potential to hook me back in. The door was open for me to have all the noncommittal sex I wanted with a stunningly attractive woman. How is a man supposed to turn down an offer like that?

"Why don't you come over this week and we can talk about it, Birch? I have some expensive French wine that was given to me by one of my clients. We can open one of the bottles and just talk."

"I don't know, Lana, let me think about it."

"Are you engaged or anything like that, Birch?" She persisted.

"No, nothing like that."

"Come on, how about Wednesday night, about 7:30?"

"All right, let's talk about it Wednesday."

4-2 - - Sumptuosity

"Sumptuosity isn't a word, but it ought to be." - - Birch Bentley

Wednesday night Lana and I didn't even make it to end of the bottle, and it was a truly impressive Pinot Noir at its perfect age.

Lana Luscious was too much for my weakness for women to handle. I didn't care if I was being used, it felt good and as long as

I wasn't approving any overseas transactions that were illegal, nobody was getting hurt.

Jennifer wouldn't have liked it if she knew but I never said our arrangement was exclusive, although I was sure she thought it was that way.

Lana's pillow talk was the reality check that reminded me why she was doing this.

"Birch, you know Yuri has been asking me when you're going to come by and see him."

"I've been really busy at work; we're trying to put an acquisition together."

"He keeps telling me how much business he can steer your way. It would mean a lot to me if you would just talk to him."

"Sure, I'll give him a call," I conceded at last.

"Let me properly thank you, Birch, to show my appreciation."

I knew I would be getting another call from Special Agent Miller about this, but Lana was making it worth it.

4-3 - - Making Trouble & Pointing Fingers

"Blame is a monstrous creature that lives inside of words." - - Birch Bentley

"Birch, this is Jill Mahoney. Sorry to be calling you on a Sunday night." Jill sounded anxious.

"No problem, Jill, what's up?"

"I just sent you an e-mail with a link to a news story on the Orlando Sentinel website." She hesitated.

"What's it about?"

"The headline says it all: Attorney General Opens Up Investigation Of Insurance Companies Defrauding Seniors."

"Is Affluent Society mentioned?"

"Fortunately, no. The piece highlights some of the insurance companies that have already been fined hefty amounts for regulatory infractions, and how the Attorney General is working in tandem with the Insurance Commissioner to clean up the insurance industry in Florida."

"How does that affect us, Jill?"

"The way these things work is they'll dribble information. Then right before the election they'll have some big announcement. My concern is that we own a future slot on their bad insurance company timetable."

"What can we do?"

"Not much we can do at this point, Birch. I'm continuing to work with our lobbying firm to probe what can be done through our political action committee connections."

On Monday Al called me into his office after the Executive Meeting.

"Birch, look at this PM from Scott Kerr."

There was a PM circulated to the Executive Committee from Scott Kerr, head of Corporate Communications. Scott used paper because there was an unwritten company policy at the C-Suite level not to use e-mails for certain kinds of information. No sense leaving a trail for anyone to follow; so in certain sensitive situations we used a hand-written Personal Memo that was called a PM.

I read the short PM from Scott.

Please be advised of recent developments in Florida that have the potential to escalate to a crisis management level and impact our merger with ALH.

This has been escalated by the recent fiasco regarding the termination of Brad Bishop and the failure to separate Affluent Society from fraudulent activity.

A course of action is required to safeguard there is no further escalation that could impact acquisition discussions.

SK

There was no news in his PM; there was only his observation of the obvious.

I was sure he delighted in pointing out the controversy since I was at the center of it. He didn't mention my name in the PM, but the implication by Scott that this was entirely my fault wasn't lost by the key players.

Scott Kerr was not my ally; I had known that for a long time. He was my defeated rival and took every chance to take a shot at me that he could.

Years ago, Scott and I had both been selected for the Fast Start program, which involved moving people around from department to department. Some of this was to help remove the communication barriers that resulted from everyone working in their own silos. The program was also intended to help groom a pool of future executives that had working knowledge of all the parts of the company whole.

Scott was smart, but he was a weasel who couldn't be trusted, and few people liked him. Scott resented my relationship with Al Perri and was always trying to go around that link directly to Donald Hightower.

Scott was in charge of corporate communications, an important job, but not one that matched the level of Senior Vice President that I'd attained. He made less than half of what I did, which I was sure he considered a gross injustice.

I handed the PM back to Al who went directly to the shredder in his office and fed the document into the machine that chewed the paper up into little strips.

"New shredder, Al?"

"Yeah, that other one was too big and clunky; made my office look too much like an *office*."

"The color of this one goes well with the window shades, Al."

He looked at the window shades and then back at his new shredder, way too absorbed with himself to realize I was yanking his chain.

"What did the Chairman say, Al?"

"What do you think? He's focused on the ALH deal and hears someone is throwing a chair through a conference room window. Things like that make their way around more than the company grapevine. You screwed up on this one, Birch. Now there are articles being written about insurance companies cheating people. Good thing for you Affluent Society hasn't been mentioned in any."

This was so typical of corporate scapegoating. Al sent me in to be the bad guy and do the dirty work, and the fallout was all on my shoulders as if nobody else had anything to do with the decision that caused the incident.

"Look, Al, Brad Bishop is terminated, Vince Bennett has agreed to our buyout and has vacated his office already; so he is gone, and the PAC is looking to support the right people."

Vocalizing the true purpose of the campaign contribution would have been bad form, even in a conversation between just Al and I. Nobody wanted the contribution shaped in a manner that had the appearance of a payoff from our Political Action Committee to the Insurance Commissioner and Attorney General.

"I'll relay that to the Chairman; but no more soap operas, OK, Birch? Now, where are going to lunch today?"

I'd never played poker with Al but I'm sure he would have been good at it. I had no idea how to read the man, but this I was sure of: He would throw me under the bus in a second if he thought he had to. Right then, however, he needed somebody to have lunch with him so he didn't have to drink alone.

Affluent Society had an outstanding executive dining room. There were huge paintings, oversized windows that provided a view of the Manhattan skyline, white linen tablecloths, silverware that was real silver, white gloved servers; every touch you would expect and some you wouldn't.

Everything was free. The waiter or waitress gave you a little slip of paper for you to check off your salad or appetizer, entrée, and desert. There were usually about three or four choices per day in each category.

The sensation was you were breaking bread in the same manner as the Jacob Astor's and Andrew Carnegie's of old. Dining in the executive dining room was an extravaganza experience for most people they weren't going to forget.

You had to be at a certain high level to eat there, or get prior approval if you weren't on the list. Most approvals were because somebody was bringing in a big customer or an influential guest. Employees also got to eat there on the tenth, and twentieth employment anniversary, and every fifth anniversary after that.

Unfortunately, I hardly ever managed to eat there because they didn't serve alcohol and Al couldn't see the point of having lunch without several drinks. If I knew Al and Donald Hightower would both be out of the office, I would always call a Board Member and ask them to meet me there, but never more than one at a time. I didn't want to make Al and Hightower suspicious.

The lack of attention paid to the Board by Perri and Hightower was sheer negligence on their part, and left a crucial opening for me I would shortly depend on.

4-4 - - Mischief

"There are but few men clever enough to know all the mischief they do." - - Francois de La Rochefoucauld

At lunch I checked my e-mails and saw a request from Sandy to give her a call. I wanted to make the call right then and there but I knew Al hated sitting by himself. As usual, when the waiter asked us if we were ready for our check, Al ordered another double & water on the side. I knew I had at least another 30 - 40 minutes before leaving. Al loved nursing his drink after lunch and expounding on his worldly experiences.

Al was a Type A personality on speed but when you put a drink in front of him he could sit still indefinitely.

When we finally left the restaurant I told Al I had to run a few errands before going back to the office. I wanted to know why Sandy was calling and didn't want to wait until I got back.

"Hello, this is Sandy."

"Sandy, this is Birch. I got your e-mail, everything OK?"

As soon as I asked her I realized I sounded a little too eager to ask if everything was OK; almost desperate to make sure everything was stable.

She'd been slightly distant, almost approaching cold, since our Florida trip, and I didn't want anything that happened on the trip to become an issue in any way.

"I'm not sure," she said. "Scott Kerr sent me an e-mail this morning and said he was putting a routine report together on the incident in Florida regarding Brad Bishop. He wanted to see if he could ask me a few questions."

This unnerved me a bit but I regained my cool instantly; on the outside at least, so as not to upset Sandy any more than she already was.

"No worries, Sandy, just tell Scott exactly what happened from your perspective."

"Maybe not everything that happened" she said.

I took this as a good sign that she had made even a passing reference at what took place in private.

"I understand. When are you meeting with Scott?"

"Tomorrow morning, I'm leaving early today."

"Sandy, I was going to call you anyway. I wanted to review the status of our compliance files on our new disability product with you. Do you have any time tomorrow afternoon?"

"Yes, will two o'clock work?" she asked.

"I'll come down to your office. See you then."

We both knew I didn't want to talk about disability policies; we were going to hash over her conversation with Scott Kerr.

4-5 - - Mood Change

"Your silence will protect us." - - Birch Bentley

When I arrived at Sandy's office the next day at two, something had dramatically changed in Sandy's mood. Whatever happened that morning between Scott and her could not have been good.

"Birch, we have to talk," Sandy said in a whispered but firm tone, as I entered her office.

"What is it?" I asked.

"Scott Kerr was here in my office this morning for over an hour asking me all kinds of questions. I know he was fishing because some of the questions were clearly over the line and not just about what happened with Brad Bishop."

"Look, Sandy, Scott Kerr knows *nothing* about certain events and what is missing from the story will stay that way, you have my word on that."

"Maybe, but he was so obnoxious; and he is such an annoying person. And look, Birch, I have two children in private school. I need this job badly; I can't afford to have anything go haywire."

I didn't sense panic from Sandy as much as fear, combined with a determination there wasn't going to be a price to pay. There couldn't be a price to pay. Losing her job would have been a personal and family disaster.

"Sandy, I understand completely. Let me deal with Scott; you go about your work like usual and everything will be fine.

"Thanks, Birch, but let me ask you something: are *you* in trouble?"

I tried not to have a shocked look on my face at her question.

"I ask that, Birch, because there was just something about Scott's demeanor like he knew something or was up to something. The way he said your name when he was asking about you had a scoffing tone to it."

"Sandy, this competition between Scott and I goes back a while and I promise not to drag you into the struggle between us. I will deal with Scott."

4-6 - - Bull Charge

"Arrogance can be the fuel for a dangerous situation." - - Birch Bentley

I didn't waste a second after leaving Sandy's office. I took the elevator to Scott's floor and gathered my poise on the way up.

I saw Scott in his office and since he wasn't on the phone I walked right past his secretary into his office. He was subordinate to me, and I didn't want to defer to him in any way. I was the alpha-male between the two of us and I wanted to reestablish the pecking order and make him feel his secondary status.

I walked in and stood over his desk, like a Dad does when he comes home from work and you're in trouble. I almost had my nuts up on the top of his desk.

"Scott, do you have a minute?" I asked.

"For you, Birch, always."

"Great, may I?" I pointed toward one of the two chairs in front of his desk.

"By all means," he gestured back.

I removed my nuts from the close proximity of his desk.

"Al told me yesterday that you raised some concerns about what happened in Florida, and I wanted to see if there was any information that I could provide?"

This was strategic. I was letting him know that Al confided in me by showing me the PM Scott had written. It also deflected any attention away from Sandy.

"Just routine," said Scott. "You know how stories go around, and I wanted to be sure we were out ahead on this one in case there's a need to spin events in some way."

Dimwit; you don't admit that you may spin a story. Not to anybody. When you do, you say something public about your integrity. Other people spin stories, never you.

"Is there anything about what happened that I can shed any particular perspective on?" I asked.

"Since you're here, why don't you run down your version of events with me - if you don't mind?"

"Not at all, and there isn't that much to tell. I went to Florida to terminate Brad Bishop and his immediate superior due to irregular marketing practices. While I was there I met with the Florida Insurance Department officials to make sure there wasn't going to be any fallout over the matter; plain and simple."

"And Sandra Lockheart went with you?"

"Yes, she has long-standing relationships with the people in the Florida Insurance Department as a result of her compliance duties and I thought her presence would be of help."

"Well, Birch, it's like you say, pretty plain and simple, and I really appreciate you coming up to add your perspective."

"No worries" I said. "Let me know if you need anything else."

I really hated this guy. They say the opposite of love is not hate, it's indifference, which is what I feel about most people that annoy me, just indifference. Hate requires an investment of my emotions; a waste of my energy and resources.

Scott reminded me of the Cassius character out of Shakespeare's Julius Caesar when Caesar says to Mark Antony: *'he has a lean and hungry look and thinks too much. One who hears no music and sees no plays and when he smiles, it is as if he mocks.'*

Shakespeare described Scott Kerr perfectly. He had a crooked smile that looked like there was a sneer hiding behind it. It was an insincere menacing smile.

I was determined to figure out a way to deal with this dangerous pain in the ass when the time was right, so I wouldn't have to waste another second on him.

There was an unknown that was bothering me. I knew Scott had a backchannel to Hightower. What I didn't know for sure, but what now seemed likely was that he also had a backchannel to Al Perri.

4-7 - - PAC Relief

"If someone knows more than they should; take it as a warning something is amiss." - - Birch Bentley

I went up to legal and I could see that Jill Mahoney was on the phone. I motioned that I needed to come in and talk to her, and she promptly finished her phone call and invited me in.

"Birch, I figured I'd be hearing from you soon."

"Why is that, Jill?"

"Scott Kerr was here, wanting to know more about the PAC contributions that were being considered for the Florida Insurance Commissioner and Attorney General; said he wanted to be out in front of all the information."

This Scott Kerr just couldn't help himself and was really starting to piss me off. He should have read Colin Powell's principle about not starting a war you weren't prepared to win.

"How did he know there were campaign contributions being considered?" I asked.

"I don't know" said Jill. "I just assumed you had told him."

Scott knew more than he should for his position.

"What did you tell him?" I asked.

"I didn't tell him anything; the only conversation I've had about this besides you is Al Perri. I told him that we're working through the political relationships of the PAC Committee to let the AG and Insurance Commissioner Campaigns know we have expressed some interest in supporting the good work they are doing to protect the citizens of Florida."

"Or something like that," I added. "Is there anything else Scott said or I should know?"

"No, not really, that's all there is right now. These things work slowly but the process is effective."

"Jill, great, thanks for updating me - and keep up the good work."

On the way back to my office I mentally made a short list of who might be feeding Scott Kerr information. There weren't too many options: was Hightower his source or were Hightower and Perri both blabbermouths?

I don't like to think of Scott as a rival because he's such a dickhead. At this point we both knew I was ahead in position and influence; but there was jeopardy to being out ahead with a knife-thrower at my back. He was probably viewing his star rising partly through the same method that my own star had risen; the involuntary vacating of the people ahead of me. If he could get rid of me that would be one less person between him and the top.

4-8 - - Settle, No Matter What

"I don't care what it takes; what I don't need now are complications." - - Birch Bentley

Jennifer was changing my world view as I arrived at work on Wednesday. Monogamy didn't seem like the prison it did before. It seemed more like a safe place where two people could go and be happy, protected by a bubble of trust that could not be pierced by anyone else.

Lana didn't really enter into that equation because that was just sex.

Unfortunately, the bliss didn't have much of a chance to set in.

I was looking at an e-mail from Jill Mahoney. She had heard from attorneys representing Brad Bishop.

I immediately called Jill.

"Jill, talk to me. Where are we at with this Brad Bishop affair?"

"Looks like Brad Bishop and friends want to play hardball," Jill said. "We have a wrongful termination lawsuit."

"That is complete and utter *bullshit*," I said.

As I said it I realized I had mouthed almost the exact words to describe the situation that Brad Bishop had used back in Vince Carter's office.

"I agree; if we want to fight this, we'll win."

"Settle, Jill, we can't afford to have that kind of lawsuit hanging out there. Play it smart, but settle, and settle quickly."

"Message delivered, message received, Birch."

I immediately went over to Al's office and did manage to briefly relay to him my conversation with Jill about Brad Bishop. Al kind of nodded that settling was the right thing to do, but all he really wanted to do was tell me about the girl he met the night before and was having lunch with today.

"Birch, this girl is really something and has money out the Wazoo. Her husband apparently has a new girlfriend and she doesn't intend to get left behind in the romance department. Let's just say she was able to add a point to her side of the ledger last night."

"Too much information, Al. Where are you taking her to lunch today?"

"Down to SOHO for some sushi, and by the way, don't expect me back this afternoon."

"Al, from the way you're talking, sounds like you're already thinking about breaking your three and out rule."

"This might be the exception, this might be the exception."

4-9 - - A Botch Of Epic Proportions

It's OK to have a tiger by the tail: provided you know what to do next." - - Unknown

By the next week just as things had settled down total chaos broke out.

Jill called me and before I had a chance to answer I saw that Al was calling in at the same time.

I decided to take Jill's call first, in case she had information that would help me better deal with Al.

"Birch, sorry to have to wreck your morning like this, but there are more problems. There's an editorial in the Orlando Sentinel about the Florida Attorney General doing backroom deals in exchange for campaign contributions and Affluent Society Insurance is mentioned."

"I'm guessing our PAC has already contributed to the campaigns?"

"Yes, late last week. Scott Kerr is working with our PAC on the press release."

My hairs bristled every time I heard the name Scott Kerr.

"How much did we contribute?"

"Not that much. $60,000.00 to the AG, and another $40,000.00 was sent to the Insurance Commissioner's campaign."

"That doesn't seem like that big a deal."

"Their political opponents are raising a ruckus and framing the contributions as buying influence. The implication is the AG and Insurance Commissioner are in the pockets of the insurance companies." Jill said this as if she was trying to sound indignant.

I had no idea how the press could come up with a wild accusation like that.

"What about Brad Bishop? Has that been settled?" I asked.

"There is some good news. We're set to settle on the extremely low side: only $35,000.00, plus $15,000 in legal fees. But I hope his attorneys aren't reading the paper today, because if they are, they're going to know they have us over a barrel."

"OK, it is what it is. I'll get back to you."

I walked over to Al's office and the Chairman was in talking with Al. It was not a good sign that the Chairman had come to Al. I sat down in the waiting area like some new job applicant and waited for Al and the Chairman to finish.

The Chairman didn't even acknowledge me as he walked by, obviously in a foul mood with his entire head an intense shade of ripe red pepper.

"Birch, how did you fuck this up so bad?" Al asked me when I was in his office.

He didn't want an answer just then; he wanted to roll out the litany of my screw ups.

"You fucked up getting rid of those sorry asses in Florida, you fucked up with the regulators, and you may have fucked up the deal with ALH."

Al's use of the F word only put an exclamation point on the realization that my own ass was really on the line here and I better think of something quick. In my opinion I hadn't screwed up anything, but my opinion wasn't what really mattered because right now what was needed was a scapegoat.

"Al, think about this. I didn't break any regulations selling policies in Florida, I terminated the problem. I didn't start the investigations in Florida; I managed them and the decisions on the contributions were made through our PAC."

Al was enraged.

"Bullshit, Birch; if you didn't screw this up, why is the Chairman all over my ass about articles in the newspapers and the ALH deal going to hell in a hand basket? You have an answer for that?"

I didn't have an answer because things were like Al said; a bit of a mess. The Chairman was on Al and Al was on me and I realized this was kind of the "Buck Stops Here" in reverse with me holding the blame bag.

"Am I fired, Al?" I asked.

"No, but you are dangling by the thinnest of threads. If the Chairman decides that heads are going to roll, I don't know who's going to be at the front of the line, you or me. Now leave me alone, I'm sure the Chairman doesn't have everything out of his system and will be coming back any minute to ream me out for the third time this morning. I've never seen him so pissed."

This was unsettling because Al was the armor I counted on to deflect any irrationality Hightower might direct my way. I had no illusions. Al wouldn't hesitate a minute to surrender me to save his own ass. I was vulnerable at this point; hanging out there with someone else controlling my fate.

I didn't like feeling this exposed and defenseless and knew I had to do something immediately before anything else happened that would affect my career.

This would have been a good time for the counsel of a best friend, but I didn't have one.

I called up Jennifer.

"Hey, Jen, do you have a minute?"

"Of course."

"I'm at a literal crossroads moment where my entire career could depend on what I do next."

"How can I help, Birch?"

"I'm trying to decide whether to be bold or cautious."

"What would your Sun character do in your situation?"

"It's Sun Tzu and thanks, you're wonderful. I'll call you tomorrow."

4-10 - - Slaying The Dragons

"If one man slay another of set purpose, he himself may rightfully be slain. He who relies solely on warlike measures shall be exterminated; he who relies solely on peaceful measures shall perish." - - The Art Of War by Sun Tzu

I retreated to my office to review my options.

If they were going to fire me, I wouldn't be without a lucrative golden parachute exit package. I could invite Jennifer to take six months off with me and live on a sailboat in Saint Augustine, or somewhere else quiet and beautiful.

We'd be together, out of the way where we could just be with each other, and let the rest of the world go right on doing their thing without us. Breaking off the grid and making our own grid.

I wasn't quite ready for that extreme. There was too much money to be made at the top. I *did* have a risky plan to salvage my career and life-style in ready.

I opened my iPad and looked at my list of options for exactly this type of situation and played with the various scenarios in my mind. I had labeled this list 'Taking The Money Shot.'

I had no empathy for Al and Hightower for what I was about to do. Everyone knows: if you live by the sword, you die by the sword. The bastards had cut the nuts off a lot of people on their way to the top and deserved anything they might get. Right below where I had typed 'Taking The Money Shot' were the words, 'one must not have pity for a snake.'

I read my quote and was suddenly reminded of a dream I had the previous night and not remembered until right then. In the dream I was hiking in the woods and came upon a snake. My father warned me to stay away and so I started off in the direction of a right angle to where the snake was lying. Instead of just remaining coiled, the snake came after me. I started running but the snake was fast and was gaining on me and I was worried I would fall down. I didn't remember what happened in my dream

after that but the relativity to my situation at Affluent Society was not lost on me.

I logged on to Travelocity, avoiding our corporate travel site, and booked myself on the next flight to Little Rock. With the time change, I would be arriving shortly after lunch, Central Time. I sent a personal e-mail to Ramsey Layne.

Dear Mr. Layne,

I am flying to Little Rock today specifically to see you and would appreciate a few minutes of your time to address some provocative information concerning a potential transaction with Affluent Society. I should be arriving a little before noon CST.

Sincerely,
Birch Bentley
Senior Vice President
Affluent Society Insurance

Then I logged on to the master drive and found the most current contract negotiations with ALH. I printed out a copy to study on the airplane and headed to JFK.

I rented a car in Little Rock and went directly to the ALH Headquarters to see Ramsey Layne. I was informed that he was at his club, and would be expecting me.

When I arrived at the Sterling Country Club, the surroundings were exquisite. I knew there were numerous millionaires in the Little Rock area, generated from the wealth effect of Walmart. Sterling was the most exclusive club to get into. Not quite on par with Augusta with name recognition, but it lacked nothing else by comparison.

"Mr. Layne, my name is Birch Bentley and I'm a senior vice-president at Affluent Society Insurance. Would you extend me the courtesy of 20 minutes of your time? I feel certain it will be a profitable decision for you."

Ramsey Layne was 66 and other than his solid grey hair, looked like he was in his early fifties. He was the founder of ALH and had

built a small start-up insurance company into a multi-billion dollar organization. He was powerful, rich, still attractive, and intimidating.

He was sitting with his second in command, Vic Remfield, and they each had an ice tea in front of them.

"I know of you, Mr. Bentley. Please sit down and tell me what this is all about?"

"Sir, if I may ask you to suspend any thoughts regarding whether I am being loyal or disloyal until I finish, let me share some information with you."

I went through the big picture of the merger proposal. I explained what happened in Florida. I shared my thoughts about the synergy of the two companies merged together.

I explained my positioning with the Affluent Society Board of Directors and how many would back me and what would entice Al and the Chairman to walk away.

I discussed my theory about the changing insurance distribution models and how data analytics could be used to maximize the value of each customer by predicting their needs and future purchases. Not too dissimilar from another Arkansas company that had used technology as one of their tools to dominate in a different industry; retail.

I told him my beliefs about insurance companies forming strategic alliances with non-traditional organizations to expand distribution; possibly with the biggest retailer in the world located right there in Arkansas.

I justified why I thought the shares of the combined company would rise in price, and what that would mean for his own shares and those of the people and institutions that were invested in the two companies.

When I finished, he said: "Mr. Bentley, let's go back to my office. There are some of my key people there I want you to meet."

I flew back to New York that night exhausted but exhilarated, feeling close to victory, but knew defeating Hightower and Perri wasn't over yet.

I called Sean on his mobile phone.

"Sean, this is Birch, sorry to be calling you so late."

"That's OK, I'm glad to hear from you. Al Perri called me twice this afternoon to see if I could locate you."

With Al this could have meant anything from he wanted to go chasing and drinking after work to come into his office so he could fire me.

"Sean, I wanted to ask if you could come into work at 6:00 a.m. tomorrow."

4-11 - - The Board

"He who is prudent and lies in wait for an enemy who is not, will be victorious." - - Sun Tzu

I arrived at work the next morning at 6:00 a.m., well before Al or the Chairman would be there. I quickly went to work and faxed the letter I had received from Ramsey Layne to all the Board Members.

To The Affluent Society Insurance Board of Directors,

I am advising you to the intentions of Arkansas Life & Health in regard to our most current merger discussions.

I am formally requesting that you hold a Board Of Directors Meeting as soon as reasonably possible regarding the proposal to merge Affluent Society Insurance and Arkansas Life & Health.

If you can establish a quorum, we will accept in principle the last offer proposed to ALH for the merger of the two companies.

Once the merger is finalized, I am requesting your support for voting me the Chairman of the Board of the combined company. I

134

intend to use our board seats to vote for Birch Bentley as the new President of the combined company and ask for your support in that vote as well.

I have sent a private communication to Donald Hightower and Al Perri explaining an exit package our Board representatives would agree to that I think they will find is more than fair.

All of us At Arkansas Life & Health look forward to a profitable future relationship.

Sincerely,

Ramsey Layne
CEO
Arkansas Life & Health

By the time Al Perri and Donald Hightower arrived at their offices, they were toast. They could either explain why it was more important for them to keep their jobs and risk the merger; or they could keep their mouths shut, take the substantial amount of money they were being offered, and run, with zero to worry about.

The greedy son-of-a-bitch bastards weren't about to jeopardize the money on the table. They could count the Board votes as well as I could.

4-12 -- Al Perri

When I found the information from Ramsey Layne on my fax machine and in my e-mail, I called up Donald Hightower at his home in the Hamptons.

"Donald, this is Al Perri. Have you looked at your e-mail or walked by your fax machine?"

"Not yet, why?"

"That ungrateful piss ant Birch Bentley is in bed with Ramsey Layne to make a play for the company."

"What, how?"

"He has a buy-out planned for you and me and he's already contacted everyone else on the Board to try to get them to go along with the deal."

"I don't understand, Al, what deal?"

"Ramsey Layne is going to be CEO of the new combined company, Vic Remfield is going to be the Vice-CEO, and Birch Bentley is going to be made president."

"That can't be right."

"It is, check your e-mail or fax, and if the Board goes along with what's being proposed by Ramsey Layne, then it will become official."

"What kind of offer are they making us?"

"A sweet one."

"I know I don't have to tell you this, Al, but if you talk to anybody tell them no way. They didn't make us their best offer on their first try. There is no way I am out, but if I am it's going to be with a big bag of money."

"Of course. Donald, I've been counting the votes in my head and I think we only have three of the seven we need. You, me, and your college buddy. After that we're left holding our dicks."

"Not our dicks, Al, big bags of money. Remember, they don't want trouble, they just want the company. A two billion dollar enterprise has lots of money on the table to make this happen quick and easy."

"OK, how about I drive up to your place this morning and we can discuss it in private?"

"Good, I'll have my private attorney stand by to take our call when we're ready to talk with him."

Scott Kerr

This morning I went up to Donald Hightower's office and was told he would not be coming into the office and all inquiries should be directed to Birch Bentley.

Inquiries about what?

Something was up, and as the Director Of Communications I should be the first to know - but nobody had told me anything.

I went down to Al Perri's office and was told the same thing.

I called Jill Mahoney in legal and she wasn't talking. I couldn't tell if she had been muzzled or just didn't know anything.

I heard some commotion outside my office and saw Birch Bentley standing there with two of our security people.

4-13 - - One Final Thing To Do

"If you prick us do we not bleed? If you tickle us do we not laugh? If you poison us do we not die? And if you wrong us shall we not revenge?" - - William Shakespeare

Things were working out. Perri & Hightower were filthy rich and looked like geniuses for pulling off the merger. They weren't about to try and do battle with the Board when they could walk away with millions in their pockets. They did, however, each manage to negotiate to remain on the Board of Directors.

I was President of the company, and I didn't have to go out drinking with Al all the time, which meant I could spend more time with Jennifer. Brenda had moved out of Jennifer's place so that distraction was easier to put out of my mind.

Someone had jokingly called me 'The Presinator.' Everyone knew I had successfully pulled a coup. Someone else called me 'The Insuranator,' and there was an e-mail going around with a poll question about which one was the best choice. I kind of liked 'The Insuranator' but I pretended the attention was no big deal.

The business press picked up the account and gave me some publicity. The narrative was a good offbeat story to write, but I turned down the interview request. I didn't want the publicity; I wanted the job and the money.

There was one more thing 'The Insurinator-In-Chief' had to do.

"Sean, could you ask Lance Rettberg from security to come up to my office with the two biggest guards we have, and for each to bring two banker's boxes?"

When the two security men arrived at my office, I couldn't contain my self-satisfaction as I said, "Gentlemen, follow me." I paraded past as many offices as I could before arriving at Scott Kerr's office.

I saw Scott look up at me and then the two security men. He had a puzzled look on his face as he saw me through his glass partition wondering what I was up to approaching his office with two security officers.

"Scott, these two gentlemen are going to pack your things for you and escort you downstairs. We're reorganizing the PR department and eliminating your position.

I savored the shocked and helpless look on Scott's face. Going forward there would be no knives in the back to worry about; at least not from Scott Kerr.

I told him we were reorganizing his department rather than firing him to reduce the risk of another wrongful termination suit, although I was sure he would file one.

Letting him go because his position was eliminated due to reorganization rather than firing him would make the eventual settlement we would have to make smaller. Employers often make the mistake of firing someone and find themselves in court, when they would have so much more of a defensible position if they simply reorganized and eliminated or combined a job function.

There was usually some type of severance pay at Scott's level, but there would be no fat exit package for Scott Kerr other than

the eventual settlement. He would have to explain to any future employer why his department was reorganized and he was the one who was out.

In ancient Rome the generals would return from a victorious campaign with much fanfare and parade into the city with the captured slaves and plundered treasure in tow. This was their glory. The removal of Scott Kerr in this sense was my victory march; and while I normally had no need for personal glory, I couldn't resist this one imprudence.

I had that coming to me and so did Scott Kerr.

I went back to my office and Sean informed me that Ramsey Layne was on hold waiting for my return.

"Mr. Layne, how are you today?"

"Birch, I'm doing fine. I wanted to speak with you a minute about the next Board Meeting. Can you be sure that we have a copy of the agenda at least a week ahead of time so we can be sure to not miss any items, suggest any loose ends that we need to tie up on our end, things like that."

"Yes, I'll make sure Sean has that to your office with plenty of time for your review, and can I take a minute to thank you one more time for your support and faith in me? I know you won't be disappointed."

"Birch, I'm sure I won't be disappointed and I look forward to seeing you in New York. Goodbye."

As I started to disconnect, I heard roaring laughter as Ramsey Layne was ending the call and repeating "I'm sure you won't disappoint me, Birch" to what must have been a number of other people in the room with him.

I wondered what was so funny?

To Be Continued...

Thank you for reading Birch Bentley: Lies That Glitter - Book 2

To request a a list of all the Bentleyisms send an e-mail to walt@waltbernard.com and just put Bentleyisms in the subject line.

One last request. It is very helpful to me, as well as other readers, if you would take a minute to write a review on Amazon, or your other favorite review sites. It is very appreciated.

I have attached the Preface from the second book of the series below. It may help you to decide whether to continue to read the Birch Bentley series.

There is also a picture of each cover in the series and the names of the major sections of each book

Thank You & Best Wishes,

Walt Bernard

Preface

Birch Bentley: Unexpected Forces - Book 2

**Unexpected forces have the potential
to raze all that is in their path.**

Man plans and God laughs.

We've all experienced it, or at the very least, seen it happen to others. We plan, strategize and project outcomes that will never come to pass.

Sometimes we're the problem, sometimes it's outside influences we never anticipated, but it doesn't matter. It is what it is.

Some surrender at the first sight of what seems like unsolvable challenges and problems.

The tough-minded don't always see the need to capitulate. They are determined to either right the ship or go down with it.

When we see someone pull off a victory under these circumstances, we have a story of worthwhile achievement that merits our attention.

Which of these two approaches is best? Who can say, but there seems to be something about our character, or maybe it's something in our genes that dictates which path we choose.

Perhaps it's our destiny that pulls us in one direction or the other.

If you're reading this sequel to "Birch Bentley: Lies That Glitter - Book 1" you are most likely the kind of person that doesn't give up easily and enjoys reading about someone succeeding against overwhelming odds.

You're a "fighter" and you appreciate the "fight" in Birch Bentley even though you may not always condone his methods.

You already know you aren't like a lot of your peers. Your difference is on the inside of you. When you learn how to 'let it out' if you haven't already done so, you will amaze yourself.

There may be a limit to what you can achieve but there's no limit to what you can dream. Don't let your dreams die, and if they have, rekindle them. Everyone faces the same battles you do – get down to work, fight your battles, and win.

Here is how C.S. Lewis said it.:

The only people who achieve much are those who want knowledge so badly that they seek it while the conditions are still unfavorable. Favorable conditions never come." - - C.S. Lewis

If your conditions aren't favorable; don't stop, don't wait, pursue your dreams anyhow. Have the faith to believe in your dreams and the will to achieve them.

Best Wishes,

Walt Bernard

Book 1

BIRCH BENTLEY

Lies That Glitter

Walt Bernard

He wants it all; it burns in his soul.

Unexpected forces can be swift and unforgiving.

Book 3

BIRCH BENTLEY
Boardroom Checkmate

Walt Bernard

Nobody should ever be surprised when the cupboards are bare; emptied by the people who were sworn to stock them and keep them stocked.

145

Book 4

BIRCH BENTLEY
Trouble FInds Him

Walt Bernard

Does Birch find trouble or does trouble just find him?

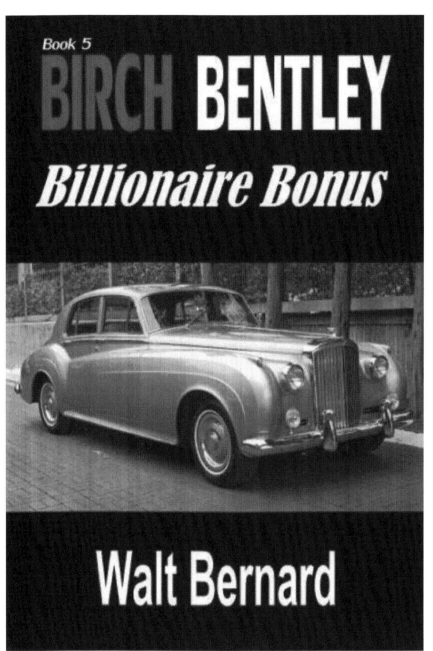

Book 5

BIRCH BENTLEY

Billionaire Bonus

Walt Bernard

Birch's billionaire friends want to help make him rich. What could possibly go wrong?

**The Chinese play by a different
set of rules; 36 of them.**

Other Books Published By *I*proficiency

(All books sold on Amazon)

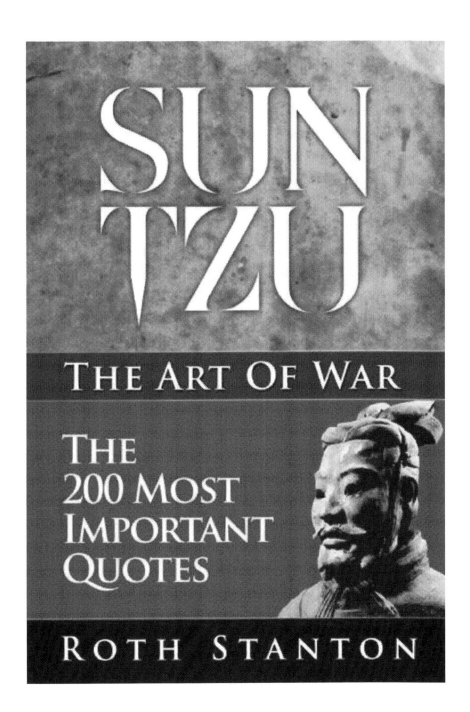

SUN TZU

THE ART OF WAR

THE 200 MOST IMPORTANT QUOTES

ROTH STANTON

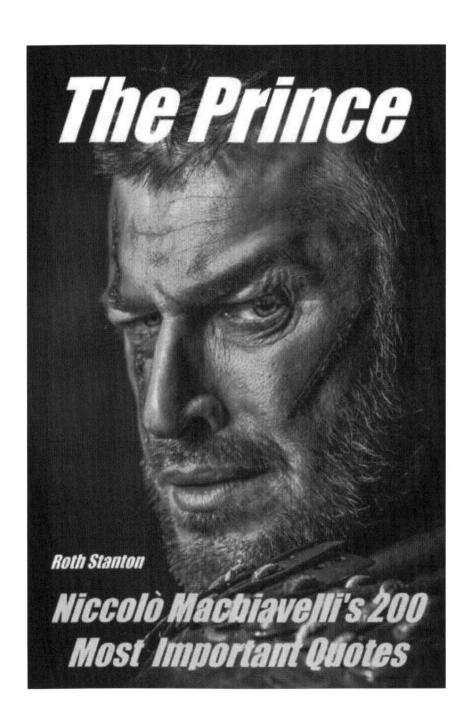

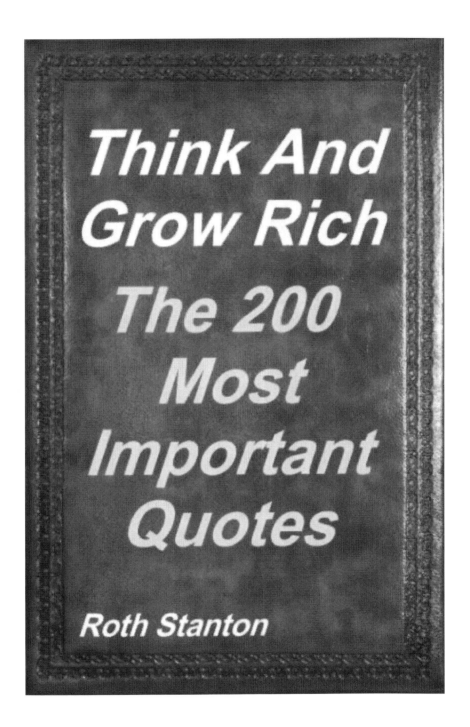

Think And Grow Rich

The 200 Most Important Quotes

Roth Stanton